Joe
The Engineer

Joe
The Engineer

Chuck Wachtel

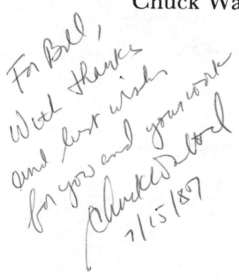

For Bill,
With thanks
and best wishes
for you and your work

Chuck Wachtel
7/15/87

Marion Boyars - London - New York

First published in Great Britain in 1985
by Marion Boyars Publishers Ltd
24 Lacy Road, London SW15 1NL.

Distributed in Australia by
Wild & Woolley Pty Ltd, Glebe, N.S.W.

Distributed in New Zealand by
Benton Ross, Auckland.

First published in the United States in 1983
by William Morrow and Company Inc. New York.

A section of this book first appeared in *Sun* magazine.

I wish to thank Robin Messing for her energy and help.

British Library Cataloguing in Publication Data
Wachtel, Chuck.
   Joe the Engineer.
   I. Title
   823'.914[F]   PS3573.A29

ISBN 0-7145-2831-5

Typeset in 12pt Baskerville by Photosetting, Yeovil, Somerset.
Printed and bound in Great Britain by
Biddles Ltd, Guildford and King's Lynn

For Mrs. Nettie Rizzotti

There can be a brick
In a brick wall
The eye picks

GEORGE OPPEN

part one

July 6–13

1

JOE THE ENGINEER and Joe Flushing Avenue are driving out to Howard Beach, the neighbourhood whose water meters they were assigned to read that morning. They're wearing dark green shirts with the letters B/Q in two-chambered patches over the left breast pockets, and flashlights, which hang from leather grommets that slip onto their belts. They are what Brooklyn/Queens Water Resources call a Meter Sector team. Each working day they drive out to a different ten-square-block piece of one of these boroughs, read as many water meters as its tenants, superintendents and German shepherds will allow, drive back to the office on Myrtle Avenue and wait around until it's time to punch out.

Joe The Engineer's twenty-seven and has been on the job since he was discharged from the army five years ago. Joe Flushing Avenue is fifty-four.

Joe The Engineer has been silent, looking out the passenger window at the bars, used-car lots, fast-food restaurants and yellow-painted curbs of the bus stops that line Cross Bay Boulevard. Occasionally he flips down the sun visor and checks their progress on the map folded to the South Queens area and held on by two rubber bands. They're a half inch from a darkened area about the size of a postage stamp with today's date on it. He's bored to anger with the job and has been for the last four and a half years. It's Wednesday, July 6, 1977, and it's hot and clear.

'Look,' from Joe Flushing Avenue, who does not like the silence, 'you may not like the job but it coulda been a helluva lot worse. If ya weren't a vet you'da had to start where *I* did...' This is one of Joe Flushing Avenue's favorite things to say to Joe The Engineer. '... Turnin off hydrants out in Bed-Stuy, an you ain't never seen how mad them bastards can get when somebody closes down their beach on a hot day.'

Joe The Engineer's staring out the window at a chubby teenage girl in a tight black T-shirt with the words *Handle With Care, Air Mail, Special Delivery* and *Fragile* zigzagging in silver all over it.

It's been a while and he still hasn't said anything and Joe Flushing Avenue is beginning to take the silence personally.

'Look. It's a job. Ya get a check every week. Ya got a TV, an air conditioner, money in ya pocket. That ain't enough? Ya think ya shit don't stink?'

'It's a job.'

2

JOE THE ENGINEER'S sitting on one of the two toilets in the
men's room of Mary's Bar and Grill trying to figure out
why some things stick in his mind while others pass freely
and, dammit, untraceably out of it. He's trying to
remember the whore he visited every night and sometimes
day for the three months he was stationed at a fire base just
outside Da Nang. He's trying to remember her face,
rocking rouged and sweaty, just under his, and the
sucking-farting sound he knew to be his cock, making and
breaking a vacuum inside her, and the smell of the French
perfume he bought her in Cholon, and cunt, and army cot
canvas. Now, after work, six beers into a Wednesday night,
staring down at his shoes, his pants piled around his ankles,
the black and white floor tiles, he needs to, but can't
goddammit, remember her.

And then there are the things that come into his mind as
easily as the graffiti and toilet paper on the wall right in
front of him. A month after his discharge and about two

months since he'd last seen that now, dammit, unrecallable whore, he married Rosie and spent a week in a small honeymoon lodge in the Catskills. It was where her parents had spent their honeymoon. One morning, while Rosie wrote thank-you cards to friends and relatives, Joe went for a walk. He walked back and forth along a stream that fed a small man-made lake. There were no honeymooners strolling along the path around the lake. If you're going to have your honeymoon in the Catskills or Niagara Falls and if you love the outdoors, you should get married in June. The other newlyweds were bouncing their canopied double beds, or sipping Bloody Marys in the cocktail lounge, or drifting around the indoor pool on love rafts, double-sized air mattresses, supplied by the management at no extra cost. A lot had happened in the two years since he got his draft notice. A lot more, it seemed to him, than had happened in the twenty years that came before them. He was beginning the painful adjustment to a slower and more evenly paced arrival of events. He could feel his stomach muscles begin to loosen. He sat at the spot where the stream entered the lake through a grating tangled with branches and other debris. He watched the water flow. He watched the leaves and twigs get tangled in the grating. Lodged next to each other in the branches were a child's sneaker, a dead tortoise and a Reddi Wip can. He stared at these objects briefly, unaware that later on their image would enter his mind, time and time again, without reason or conjuring, as easily as the things that were really there.

That's what he's seeing now, sitting, elbows on knees, on the bowl in the men's room of Mary's Bar and Grill. A child's sneaker, a dead tortoise and a Reddi Wip can. Of all the billions of things that can float down a fuckin river, how did those three end up next to each other? *Beats the hell outta me.*

He stands up, wipes himself, goes to the sink and washes

up. A child's sneaker, a dead tortoise and a fuckin Reddi Wip can. *Beats me.*

Joe The Engineer leaves the men's room, goes back to the bar for a last beer before going home to Rosie and dinner, tells Mary, 'Jesus, it sure stinks in the bathroom, you should throw a coupla buckets of ice into the urinals.'

Joe got the name 'Engineer' in high school when he decided that an engineer was what he wanted to be. He made the decision suddenly one night while reading Thomas Hardy's *The Return of the Native* for an English class and had come across the word 'engender.' He had no idea what it meant, so he looked it up in a dictionary. The definitions offered were 'to beget; to produce; to cause to exist.' Having even less grasp on the word than before he looked it up, he lost interest. His eyes glided down the page and landed on 'engineer':

> **en-gi-neer** One who designs, constructs and operates the structures, machines and other devices of industry and everyday life.

And that was it. This he had use for. Simple. A definition he could put on like a uniform. Joe memorized it and kept it close at hand to answer questions like, 'What does an engineer do, Joe, fix cars?' or, 'Ya mean ya gonna drive a train like Casey Jones?' And he'd run the definition to them, slowly and clearly, in an official tone of voice like the tone cops use to read you your rights. And his friends, thoroughly impressed and certain he would become one, added the word, or rather the title, 'Engineer' to his name.

Under his picture in the Richmond Hill High School yearbook it says:

> Joseph Lazaro
> Nickname: Joe The Engineer

Influenced by J. A. Roebling
who built the Brooklyn Bridge
Has won the JFK Physical
Fitness Award and a major
letter in gymnastics
ENGINEER

He no longer associates the 'Engineer' in his name with the 'engineer' in the dictionary. It's simply his name, simply a way of distinguishing him from the other Joes in the neighborhood.

On his way home Joe stops off at the A&P. He picks up a loaf of bread, some Oreos and a bottle of Pepsi. While the cashier is ringing them up, he pulls a *TV Guide* off the rack behind the register and notices that the same face, Kojak's, is on the cover of the one he already has at home.

'Hey, this is last week's.'

'New ones come out on Thursday.'

She's eighteen or so and looks bored. She has short brown hair held off her forehead by two small yellow barrettes. When a few strands, heavy with sweat, fall across her forehead, she extends her lower lip and blows them out of her eyes. According to her A & P tag she's called Denise.

She leans over the cash drawer to make change, and Joe peeks down her blouse.

'Thursday you said. That's tomorrow.'

'Yeah, every week. Right after Wednesday.'

He wants to reach in and touch her breasts. They're small and much paler than her face and arms. They seem so fragile he wonders if they sometimes hurt her.

3

ROSIE'S WAITING for Joe to walk in before throwing the shell macaroni into the boiling water. She pulls one of the kitchen chairs out from under the table, sets a portable TV on it and turns on *Hawaii Five-O*. She throws a little salt and a drop of olive oil into the water, stirs the sauce and waits. From outside she hears the bells of an ice-cream truck.

She met Joe during their freshman year at Queensborough Community College where she was studying English literature and Joe, engineering. He dropped out in the middle of his third semester and within three months was in boot camp. Many of the guys he'd gone to high school with were already *in* and, besides, he'd lost interest in college life. He found the students boring and couldn't trace any connection between the ability to read Albert Camus or dismantle a compound fraction that looked like The Flying Wallendas and the ability to design and construct the Brooklyn Bridge.

She went on to Queens College and nearly finished her B.A. when, five years ago, at his welcome home party at Mary's, Joe asked her to marry him right away. They decided she would finish up later on when they could afford it.

'Don't worry,' Joe told her, 'there's gonna be at least one member of the Lazaro family with a college education.'

Her parents opposed the marriage. All they knew about Joe (they'd met him less than a half-dozen times before his induction) was that he was a second-generation Sicilian and that he refused to speak a word across a dinner table. Then he comes home, no job, no prospects, nothing, and wants to marry their youngest daughter.

A month later Rosie told her father that she and Joe had found an apartment and ordered a bedroom set, on installments, from Mays, so he accepted the unpreventable, catered an enormous affair at Stallone's on Rockaway Boulevard, gave the bride and groom a generous envelope and, later that year, moved his wife and himself to a suburb outside Miami.

Rosie works lunches as a waitress in a coffee shop on Barclay Street in downtown Manhattan. She comes in at 11:00 to fill the salt and pepper shakers, sugar bowls, and the red and yellow ketchup and mustard squeezers. By noon the place is mobbed. She has eight tables and sometimes serves as many as five lunches at each one. In a good week she brings home more than Joe and works half the time.

Joe walks in, takes Rosie's waitress uniform off the back of a kitchen chair, slides the chair in front of the TV and sits. Rosie tells Joe that her friend Iris wants them to go to the movies with her and her new boyfriend on Saturday night.

'Wanna go?'

'Nah.'

'Why not? It's called *The Passenger* an it's got Jack Nicholson.'

'I don't like your college friends an I don't like artsy-fartsy movies even if they do got Jack Nicholson.'

He still refers to Rosie as a college person because she almost graduated and because she reads in bed every night.

'All you wanna do is watch television or hang out at Mary's.'

Joe responds by changing the channel.

'C'mmon, Joe...'

He settles on Channel 2. *Rhoda*.

'Shit! There's no talkin to you.'

They eat in silence. Joe staring at the TV. Rosie staring at her plate, refusing the communication implied in watching the same TV as Joe.

Rosie met Iris at Queens College while Joe was in the service. Soon after Joe and Rosie were married (Iris was a bridesmaid), she graduated and spent the next year traveling through Europe. Iris had been planning the trip, a graduation present from her parents, for her entire senior year and wanted Rosie to come along with her. Rosie decided to work for six months and then meet Iris in Rome, where she had relatives, and stay for a month or two.

She hadn't expected Joe to want to get married so soon. They had discussed it in their letters but not with the kind of urgency he had in person. Iris advised her to wait. 'Come to Europe first,' she said. 'At least graduate.' But Joe's urgency overpowered any influence her own desires or Iris's advice could have on her near future. He had been out of *the world* for too long. Out of its sense of time. When you return, what you do is get married, have children, own things, weigh yourself down, attach yourself to its surface, nestle under its wings. And you do it right away. The fathers of Richmond Hill taught their sons how to return from a war. You do it right away. And you don't think about leaving again.

Rosie and Joe were married in November. Iris left that January. For the next year they received a biweekly postcard with pictures of the Changing of the Guard, the Seine, Notre Dame, the Colisseum, the Pietà, and various paintings, landscapes and harbors. The postcards always opened with 'To Rosie and Joe,' but the contents were always for Rosie. Once Iris sent an Edam cheese from Holland. It came in a little wooden box with a note saying, 'Paid for by Jann Immer (pronounced Yon) who, for your information, is a slightly older, extremely handsome, multilingual lawyer, who I met in Delft and who is now showing me (and how!) Amsterdam.'

When they read it Rosie giggled. Joe wouldn't even taste the cheese.

After dinner Rosie clears the table cool and waitresslike and announces that she's going down the block to her sister's. As she's leaving, Joe tells her, all right, he'll go with her to the fuckin movie if it's that fuckin important.

'No thanks,' from Rosie. 'I'll go myself,' as she heads down the stairs, in no mood to be grateful.

Within half an hour Joe's walking down Atlantic Avenue toward Mary's. The largest building along that stretch of avenue is the South Queens Boys Club, a huge stone fortress originally built to house the South Queens chapter of the Knights of Columbus. It's the first structure to single itself out from the used-car lots, autobody shops and rows of two-story walk-ups, sided with the kind of green, brown or dark red gravelly shingles that have saddened the walls of South Queens since before the Second World War. A yellowish-gray band of light, where Atlantic Avenue slopes into the horizon, is all that is left of the sun,

Joe Flushing Avenue, now half smashed, is sitting at the bar where Joe left him two hours ago. Johnny Lemons, who washes floors for Mary when he's not running numbers, had bet him a beer that he couldn't remember the Boy Scout Oath. Joe Flushing Avenue is waving his fat arms around as if to push away anyone who might try to help him.

'Wait. I got it. A Boy Scout is helpful, friendly ... uh ... no no. Wait ... a Boy Scout is helpful, friendly ...'

'Horny,' from Joe The Engineer, his way of announcing himself.

'Hey Joe, wait. Don't stop me now. I'm in the process a winnin a beer from Johnny here.'

He takes a big sip, rubs his fingers under his nose and tries to sort out this list of impossible virtues in his drunken skull. He finally manages to compile a list good enough to satisfy Johnny and the contest is won.

'Joe, whaddya doin back here? Ya usually stay home once ya get there.'

'Didn't feel like watchin the tube.'

'Dja have a fight with Rosie?'

'Nah.'

Joe Flushing Avenue is on his thirteenth beer. It's easy to keep track of your beers at Mary's because every fourth is a kickback. Mary keeps score in her head. When she taps her fist lightly on the bar in front of you, you know she has just filled your fourth or your eighth or your twentieth. There have been nights when she's tapped the bar in front of Joe Flushing Avenue as many as eight times.

Joe sits down and Mary tells him he got a free one coming from before.

'Great.' He slugs it down and it finds the other seven waiting.

Joe Flushing Avenue, beginning his fourteenth beer, is

ready to talk current events.

'Remember that lady whose dog ate her baby?'

'Yeah.'

'I read in the *News* that they let her out today. Just like that. A crazy sick broad who feeds her baby to a German shepherd for lunch an they let her out. Just like that.'

'She didn't feed the baby to the dog.'

'Oh yeah?'

'She just left em alone together.'

'So what. It's still her fault. If I was that judge I'da strung her up by the tits.'

Mary refills their glasses and Joe Flushing Avenue changes the subject.

'I came on ta the Greek lady again today.'

'The Greek lady?'

'You know. The one who sells hot dogs in front a the office. The big strong one with those amazing bazoons.' He cups his hands in front of him with the fingers stretched wide enough to palm canteloupes.

Joe shakes his head.

'The one who's always standin by the subway entrance. The one Lenny calls Helen a Troy.'

'Oh yeah. Any luck?'

'Nah. She won't budge. Each time she says no, I wanna get inta her pants even more. Jeez, I bet she got muscles in her shit.'

Joe Flushing Avenue comes on to every woman within reach. He works the hit-and-miss system. He hits once or maybe twice for every four hundred misses.

'How about you? Ya gettin any?'

'Nah.'

'What are you?... a woman's man?... a Boy Scout?'

'Nah. I don't know.'

'Tell ya what... I'll fix ya up.'

'Whatamy, broken?'

'C'mon, I'm serious.'
'Shit.'
He wonders where Joe Flushing Avenue gets the nerve
to come on to so many women, especially pretty ones, him
being so fat and all. He sometimes thinks it's only the
women who have to be beautiful. Maybe the men don't
have to be. Instead, they have to know what women want.
Be stronger. Be cocksmen. Joe Flushing Avenue has
whatever it is that enables one to believe that this is the way
it is, that it's all that simple. Joe's seen him be slick and
funny with women. He's seen him move his obese meter
reader's body in ways that seem almost graceful. He shoves
his empty glass toward Mary.
'I think too much, Joe. That's why I never get laid.'

4

FRIDAY. DINNER. Joe and Rosie are eating hamburgers, french fries and corn on the cob that Linda and Frank, Rosie's sister and her husband, brought back from their vacation in New Jersey. For the past three years they've spent their two weeks' vacation in a bungalow park on the Jersey shore, and each year they invite Joe and Rosie to come along. Rosie likes the idea. Joe flatly refuses. He can't imagine himself lying around the beach for two weeks watching Frank sleep, tune in fading, static-y Met games on his transistor radio, drink beer and fart while Rosie and Linda slop oil all over themselves. No way. The corn is an enticement. It's Frank's way of showing Joe what he's missed. Last year they brought back squash.

They're watching *Bowling for Dollars*, a game show on which contestants can win a new car and as much as five thousand dollars but rarely go home with more than a set of his and hers matching beach towels and a lottery ticket. The air conditioner hums from the bedroom. Joe starts his illiiil ea

'It tastes just like the kind ya get in the A & P except the rows are all uneven and some of the kernels are white.' He's used to the all-yellow ears they get in the supermarket with the kernels set in rows like movie seats.

Rosie agrees.

From outside they hear the sound of someone sawing wood in a nearby backyard.

'Listen,' Joe says to Rosie. *'Testa di minghia... testa di minghia... testa di minghia...'*

'You're a *testa di minghia,'* she says.

Testa di minghia, head of the cock, is a phrase Joe learned at the age of five. He was watching his father saw the boards that would become the bunk beds he and his older brother were to share. His father asked him if he understood what the saw was saying and Joe said no, he didn't understand and his father said, listen... But all Joe heard was the saw biting wood.

'Listen,' his father repeated. *'Testa di minghia.* Head of the cock. Ya hear it?'

Joe listened.

'Testa di minghia... testa di minghia... testa di minghia.'

He said it with each rip of the saw, and soon Joe heard it too.

Testa di minghia.

'This is what it's tellin ya,' his father said. 'If ya stupid enough ta do shit work for a livin you're a *testa di minghia.'*

The next contestant on *Bowling for Dollars* is introducing herself into a microphone held in front of her by an unnaturally clean-cut announcer. She's up to the part where she recites the names of friends and relatives who are watching from home.

'I got Jimmy at home... my cousin Sookie... an his wife Camille... an I'd like ta say hello ta all my friends an, ha ha, enemies in my bowling league over at Pin City Lanes.'

'All my *fuckin* friends an *fuckin* enemies,' Joe mocks her. 'Don't she know that ten-fuckin-million people are watchin her?'

The phone rings. Rosie gets up and answers it.

'Hya, honey. When are we gonna have our date?' It's Joe Flushing Avenue.

'When you lose a hundred pounds and learn to sing like Frank Sinatra.' She drops the receiver onto the bureau as if it emitted a bad odor. Then, to Joe, 'Hey Abbott, it's Costello.'

Joe picks up the phone. 'Yeah?'

'I'm down at Sammy's El talkin with two a the horniest broads I ever seen.'

'You kiddin?'

'I never seen two broads needed nookie so bad.'

'You gotta be fuckin crazy.'

'Nah, I ain't. They're about maybe thirty an I think they're stewardesses or somethin. I told one of them all about ya an I swear, when she gets up ta play the juke, ya know what I do?'

'Nah, whaddaya do?' Joe looking at a kernel of corn stuck to the toe of his sneaker.

'I rub my hand over her barstool and I swear it was soaked.'

'I don't know. We're eatin.'

'Look. I coulda called anybody but I know ya really need the exercise. I tell ya what. Just come down an have a few drinks and check it out.'

'All right.' Now whispering, 'But if this is some kinda joke I'm gonna kick your ass all over Jamaica Avenue.'

Joe tells Rosie he's going over to Mary's.

'What about dessert?'

'I'll have a beer instead.'

'You have too many beers *instead*.'

* * *

Joe walks to Jamaica Avenue and takes the el train two stops to Woodhaven Boulevard. While walking the four blocks to Sammy's El, he passes a teenager pretending to fire a pistol into the driver's window of a parked car. Two of his friends sit in the front seat. He crouches slightly, imitating the semisquat stance that cops use. He likes standing in this position. He rocks and bounces and closes one eye.

'This is how he does it,' he says to his friends as Joe passes, holding an invisible .44 in both hands. 'That's why they think he's a cop.'

'Who?' from the passenger side.

'Son a Sam, asshole.'

Sammy's El is a narrow, wood-paneled cave lit by five hanging globe lights, three of which work, and two slowly spinning Rheingold clocks. Even in summer you can smell a combination of dust, beer and steam heat from half a block away. Joe Flushing Avenue jumps from his barstool so glad to see Joe that he shakes his hand, something he's never done in the five years they've known each other. Joe hadn't really given much thought to what he was doing there until now, seeing Joe Flushing Avenue behave so strangely.

'Florence, Taxi, I'd like ya ta meet my friend Joe.'

They're in their mid-forties and definitely not the stewardess type. Joe hadn't expected much, knowing that Joe Flushing Avenue's taste begins and ends with two tits, an ass and a cunt.

'Hey Sammy, a brandy for my friend here,' from Joe Flushing Avenue. 'An how about you girls? Ya ready?'

'Nah.' In harmony.

Joe Flushing Avenue buying a drink is another first.

'I'll just have a beer. Thanks.'

Joe Flushing Avenue has his arm around the one called

Taxi. She's heavy and has a wide, round face under a pile of stiff bleached hair. She has enlarged her already meaty lower lip with a wide stroke of lipstick. Barely a trace is left of what she might have looked like twenty years ago. She aims a huge pair of tits at Joe Flushing Avenue, who stares at them as if they stared back.

If Joe has anything at all to be glad about it's the fact that Joe Flushing Avenue chose Taxi. If Taxi was all he was left with, Joe would have turned on his heel and been out of the door before anyone knew he was there. If he had to handle one of them, and he decides that he won't but would have a few drinks, go home and watch Johnny Carson from the safety of his own bed, it would have to be Florence. Even Johnny Carson, he figures, has got to be better than this. But *just in case*, something in his groin is telling the rest of him, if he had to, say, if they were stuck in an elevator for two days, he could handle fucking Florence, who is slim, has a fairly nice body, but misses being attractive by ten years or so.

'That's nice,' Florence says, moving over a stool and patting the one she just left. 'Both of you being named Joe an workin together an all.'

'Yeah,' Joe Flushing Avenue shouts from behind Taxi. 'If ya need ta tell us apart, I'm Joe Flushing Avenue an he's Joe The Engineer.'

'Oh,' Florence answers him though she's looking at Joe, 'I can tell you apart.'

Joe Flushing Avenue throws a crumpled five-dollar bill onto the bar and has everybody refilled. Then, rubbing his hands together, he enters serious negotiations with Taxi.

Florence is staring at Joe. Joe's staring at the wrung-out five sitting on the bar. *That fuckin gavoon*, he thinks to himself, *if he was to put a bran-new five-dollar bill in his pocket after breakfast, by lunchtime it'd look like every bank teller, pimp, bartender, whore an loan shark livin in New York had handled it.*

Time passes.

Florence tilts her head toward Joe with a cigarette in her mouth. Joe lights it, shakes out the match, then decides to light one himself. Outside a J train rumbles by. Joe looks out the open door as if he could see it. Time passes.

'Ya married?' Florence asks.

'Yeah.' Joe hopes maybe this will put her off a little.

'How long? Ya got any kids?'

'Five years. No kids though.'

'I was married. I have a daughter too. She's twelve. Lives out in Jersey with my ex... How old are you?'

'Twenty-seven.'

'Oh,' smiling.

'What?' Joe asks, wondering if her smile constituted some kind of insult.

'I was just thinkin that you're cute. Ya have nice eyes.'

'Thanks.'

'Ya don't say much, do ya?... Always this quiet?'

'I guess.'

'Hey,' from Joe Flushing Avenue. 'I don't wanna see no empty glasses.' He pulls out another tortured five. 'Hey Sammy. Fill em up.'

Another J train goes by. Time passes.

Joe Flushing Avenue, with one hand filled with a rocks glass and the other with Taxi's thigh, is telling her his life story.

Florence asks Joe about his job. 'Do you enjoy working for, what is it, the Water Reserves?'

'No, Resources.'

'Yeah. Resources.'

'Nah.' Joe getting high finds talk coming easier. 'It's a drag. Ya go down into people's basements, read their water meters an ya write down the number a units. Say it says one thousand and thirty-one an last time it said one thousand. Ya follow?'

'Yeah.'

'Well, they get charged for thirty-one units.'

'An how much does a unit cost?'

'I don't know. I just count em. How bout you? Whaddayou do?'

'I'm a cocktail waitress in a restaurant on Fifth Avenue over by the Empire State Building. Me and Taxi useta be taxi dancers. That's how she got the name.'

'What's that... a taxi dancer?'

'We worked in a dance hall. Dja ever hear of Roseland?'

'Uh huh.'

'Well, guys'd come in an buy dance tickets. They had an orchestra an all. An when they wanted ta dance they'd come over ta us, give us a ticket an we'd dance with em.'

'Wow. I heard of em but I never knew they were called taxi dancers.'

'Yup. That's what we useta do.'

By now Joe Flushing Avenue is well into his cups. 'Hey Sammy... let's all have another. Pour yourself one too.' Then, to Taxi but loud enough for Joe and Florence, 'Hey, why don't we drive out ta the Kennedy Motor Inn. We can rent a room, buy a bottle an have a coupla laughs. I hear they got cable TV with porno shows an everything. I mean it. Right on TV. Whaddaya say?'

'I gotta better idea,' Florence says. 'Why don't we all go over ta my place. It's just a coupla blocks down the avenue.'

'Great,' from Joe Flushing Avenue. He'd fuck Taxi in the middle of the street if it meant saving thirty dollars.

The idea of going to Florence's apartment bothers Joe. Maybe Kennedy would be better. Then he remembers that it doesn't matter because he's not going anywhere. *That's right. I'm goin the fuck home! Shit!* He sits there a little higher than he thought he was. The *just in case* rises in him like a snake, then uncoils *Shit I got better things to do than sit around some fuckin apartment with Florence an Joe an that blimp Taxi.*

Florence is watching Joe. She doesn't know exactly what he's thinking but gathers the general idea from the look on his face. He's rubbing his fingers over the cigarette burns that pock the bar. He stares down the row of globe lights at a lit one that's two-thirds obscured by a broken one, forming an eclipse that's about to complete itself but never does. Florence senses that it's time to interrupt.

'It'll be great. We can play the radio an Taxi an me'll show you boys how we useta make a living.'

'Yeah,' Taxi drunkenly echoes Florence, then tries to add something else but it comes out unintelligible, as if she were underwater.

The three of them are waiting for Joe's response. Joe Flushing Avenue, because he'd rather fuck in a free bed than a thirty-dollar one any day, Florence, for obvious reasons, and Taxi, because she sincerely believes that everyone will have a good time.

They watch Joe. He's still rubbing his fingers over the cigarette burns. He looks over at the two Rheingold clocks. One says 12:55. The other says 7:15.

'Jesus. There are so many cigarette burns on this bar it looks like a fuckin population map of New York City.'

Everyone laughs.

Florence knows something has broken.

Joe concentrates on his semi-drunkenness and tries to feel it fully. *Shit. Ain't nothin wrong with gettin lit up an tearin off a piece.* He feels he's just broken down a wall that stood between himself and something else. Not something he necessarily wanted. Just something he's never had. He also feels that at this very moment, somewhere inside him, the shit is hitting the fan.

* * *

As they leave Sammy's El, Joe Flushing Avenue grabs a handful of Joe The Engineer's ass. Joe shoves him and he stumbles backward into an el pillar.

Florence lives in a narrow, four-room railroad apartment. You enter into the kitchen, then the dining room, which doesn't look as if anyone uses it, except for one chair that's been pulled out from under an old oak table and has a neat pile of panties and stockings folded on it. In the living room there's a couch, two oak end tables that match the dining room set and a big old mahogany radio, the kind, Joe imagines, people used to listen to war news over in the forties. The fourth room is a bedroom. The same linoleum, worn to a dull reddish brown from years of being washed and walked on, runs through the whole apartment. Under tables and in corners where nobody walks you can still see the original red and white floral patterns.

The four of them are in the living room. Florence turns on the old radio and is spinning the tuner in search of dance music that's the same age. Joe is sitting on the couch. Taxi and Joe Flushing Avenue are standing as if waiting for an orchestra to begin its next number. Florence finds a station playing Billie Holiday and settles on the couch next to Joe. Taxi nods to her partner and they begin a slow, rocking, grinding fox-trot that looks more like a mother rocking an impossibly huge child than a dance.

The whole apartment smells of a perfume and a kind of cooking that are completely foreign to Joe.

'How about you?' Florence asks. 'Wanna dance?' Then hums a phrase of 'This Is My Last Affair' along with Billie Holiday.

'Nah.'

'Ya like the fast stuff? I can change the station?'

'Nah.'

'Ya want me to?'

'I just don't feel like dancin.'

Joe Flushing Avenue and Taxi are standing as close as their two large bodies allow. Joe imagines them in bed with Taxi on the bottom. An elephant standing thigh-deep in water and its reflection.

'Ya like this song better?'

It's still Billie Holiday. Now singing 'Am I Blue?'

'It's okay.'

Joe Flushing Avenue and Taxi waltz into the bedroom. A moment later the bedsprings let out a noise like a dozen monkeys dying painful deaths all at once. Florence giggles and gets up to close the door. When she comes back she sits much closer to Joe.

'I can read palms, ya know. Here, gimme yours.' She takes Joe's right hand in both of hers. 'This means you're gonna have a long marriage an these little lines over here . . . these are your kids. It says you're gonna have four of em.'

'Is that all?' Joe laughs, not because it seemed funny, but because the place smells so foreign to him and because the wallpaper has become as defoliated as the linoleum and because he opened his mouth and a laugh is what came out.

She takes his left hand and places his right one on her knee. 'This means you're brave and not afraid to take chances.'

Joe's hand slides slowly up Florence's leg, taking the hem of her dress with it.

'An this means you'll have a long life . . . ' She falls slowly back still holding his left hand. His right hand reaches her garter clips and he pushes the soft cotton nipples of each clip through the metal rings that clasp them. He hooks the elastic of her panties and she unfolds like a beach chair. She lifts her ass and he pulls them off.

They kiss only once, at the beginning of a long and

frantic fuck... Joe with his shirt unbuttoned and his pants at his ankles, Florence lying in her open dress. Neither of them bother removing shoes.

Joe knows, even before the last shock of sperm, that he has to get out of there immediately.

He jumps up and begins buttoning his shirt.

'Jesus... c'mon... Joe... At least stay long enough to have a cigarette.'

Joe might have if he could stop his fingers from buttoning. It's not that he'd rather be home. It's that he has to get out.

'I don't know... I can't... I just gotta split.'

'Relax an have a cigarette. You'll feel better.' Florence is sitting up, pressing her dress closed with her folded arms. Her left stocking is gathered in a ball at her ankle.

Joe just looks at her.

'Okay babe. Maybe I'll see you again. Maybe you'll come by Sammy's some night.'

'Sure. Thanks, Florence.'

Joe flies down the stairs like a man released from jail. He walks the mile or so up Jamaica Avenue because he can't bear the idea of having to stand still on the el platform and wait for the train.

Rosie's asleep. If any time passed it happened without his knowing it. He got home too fast. It feels as if he walked out of Florence's living room and right into his own apartment, which is pitch black except for the little fish-shaped night-light in the narrow hall that separates the bedroom from the bathroom.

Among the smells of his own apartment Joe suddenly realizes that he smells of Florence's perfume. He heads for the bathroom, pulls off his shirt and throws it in the sink, runs water over it, lets it soak and takes a shower. Then dries himself, wrings out the shirt and hangs it over the shower curtain rack. He stands still for one moment and listens for Rosie's even breathing to make sure she's still asleep. Then rolls his T-shirt and jockey shorts into a tight ball, sneaks into the kitchen, stuffs it into an empty milk container in the plastic garbage can and shoves it under some napkins and corn cobs. He's still not certain that he's exorcised Florence's smell but can't think of anything else he can do. He tiptoes into the bedroom and slides into bed.

Rosie is awakened slightly by the bounce of Joe getting into bed.

'What time is it?'

'Bout one.'

Rosie falls back to sleep. Joe turns toward the open window and commands his body to lie still and wait for sleep. A light breeze breaks through the screen carrying the hum of traffic from Atlantic Avenue. It's 3:30.

5

JOE AND ROSIE are waiting for Iris and her boyfriend, Roger, on Astor Place in downtown Manhattan. They're sitting at the base of an eight-by-eight black cube, balanced on one corner on the traffic island where Astor Place, Eighth Street, Fourth Avenue and Lafayette Street converge. On one side of the cube the name Jackie is written in yellow spray paint. The tail of the 'e' is elongated into a curved arrow like a devil's tail.

Iris and her boyfriend are supposed to arrive at 7:00. They plan to have dinner at a Ukrainian restaurant Iris has been telling Rosie about for weeks, followed by the film *The Passenger* at St. Marks Cinema on Second Avenue. They came early because Rosie wanted to browse in the shops along St. Marks Place.

Whenever Joe would start thinking about the night before, say if a wave of hangover passed through him reminding him that last night was unlike most other nights, he'd step down on his mental clutch, separating today from last night like a car's engine from its wheels, and coast. He plans to coast for two weeks or so if Joe Flushing Avenue doesn't keep bringing it up. By that time it will no longer be an issue. He can think it over quickly, say to himself, *Well, I got drunk, tore off a piece, what the fuck, and that's that.* When Rosie asked him why he washed out his shirt, he told her that Joe Flushing Avenue had spilled a beer on it. She found this a thoroughly believable explanation. It's a clear, warm Saturday. A nice day for coasting.

When Joe woke that morning he wasn't totally sure he still wasn't at Florence's or if he hadn't, somehow, brought some of her home with him. Perhaps Rosie could see it on him. He watched her face as she slept to see if she sensed anything in her sleeping mind. But she couldn't. And besides, he'd showered, washed out his shirt and hid his underwear. His tracks were covered.

He remembered how he felt at thirteen after having his appendix taken out. The next morning he woke groggy, afraid of the impending surgery, then realized with utter relief that it was all over. He made a shot at feeling this kind of relief. He'd wake Rosie, get her diaphragm from the medicine cabinet and suggest a leisurely Saturday morning fuck like they haven't had in a long time. But, then again, this would make the morning seem too different. Instead, he got up, took another shower and emptied the garbage. He came close to achieving the relief he wanted, close but no cigar.

Rosie bought a pair of muslin pants in a store that sold things imported from India. Joe followed her through the shops, poking around in clothes racks or sitting down and waiting in the traditional bored-husband-shopping-with-wife position. Then Rosie would come out of a dressing room modelling a skirt or a blouse she was trying on.

'Do ya like it?'

'It's okay.'

'Just okay?'

'Yeah.'

'Yeah what?'

'If ya like it, buy it.'

'But do *you* like it?'

'It's okay.'

When they had their fill of the shops, they stopped in a little restaurant that served ice cream in twenty flavors as well as Japanese food. Rosie had a frozen yogurt, Joe, a beer. Then they strolled up and down St. Marks Place, looking at things, talking, coasting.

Rosie noticed Joe staring at a sexy teenage girl in a distractingly tight T-shirt and jeans cut halfway up her ass. She was adorning the window of a unisex haircutting shop, staring out onto the street. Rosie poked Joe. 'They don't call em barbers around here,' he said, 'they call em haircutters–did ya know that?'

As they crossed Second Avenue, a Hell's Angel turned onto St. Marks Place and fell in place about fifteen feet ahead of them. He must have weighed in at two-fifty. His arms and chest were covered with tattoos of snakes, ships, skulls and initials. He wore a sleeveless leather vest with his colors on the back–*Hell's Angels M.C. New York*. Also, boots with spurs, mail gauntlets on both hands, an earring, a nose ring and a coonskin cap.

'*Maron*,' Joe said, squeezing Rosie's hand, amazed at this Hun who had the misfortune of being born into mid-twentieth-century America. 'I bet that fat fuck's got ring around the collar.'

'SHHHHHH,' Rosie whispered, laughing. 'We're in the same borough!'

Then the Angel, walking wide-legged and lazy, dragging his heels, inhaled a can of Pepsi and flung the empty, Henry-the-Eighth style, out into the street.

It's now 7:05. No sign yet of Iris and Roger. Rosie's sitting at the base of the cube with her new pants, folded in a paper bag, on her lap. Joe's leaning against the cube facing south. He's staring at the skeleton of a new office building that's going up ten blocks or so below Houston Street. On the top there's a huge construction crane, its arms as long as the building is wide. Joe imagines it to be an enormous howitzer, larger even than the One-Seventy Five, the biggest one he'd ever seen.

After induction Joe was given an aptitude test. As a result, he was offered a choice of three fields in which to specialize: infantry, communications or artillery. A sentence in a recruiting leaflet he pulled off a rack in a post office years before made the decision for him. *Imagine the thrill of hitting a target the size of a trash can from eleven miles away!* Besides, artillery duty seemed safer than infantry, and communications could involve a year of school.

What Joe hadn't realized at the time is that you cannot see for eleven miles, and if you can't see what you're hitting and if there's actually no one specific trash-can-sized object you can draw a bead on, a *thrill* is not what you get. A thrill is what you imagine you get if you're sixteen and standing in a post office on Jamaica Avenue in Queens. What you do is fire, eject, reload and fire again and try to think of anything but what might be going on eleven miles away. Joe'd often think of the things he'd do with his whore back in Da Nang, things he'd never done before, things he could think about to keep himself from imagining a six-foot-wide scar in a patch of dried-brick pavement, where, perhaps sixty seconds before, an object the size of a trash can stopped to look up. After that Joe cannot look at something as complex and seemingly indestructible as Manhattan without calculating, at least for a moment, its total annihilation. If that crane were an immense artillery piece, and if Joe manned it, he could hold Manhattan, like an egg, in the palm of his hand.

Iris and Roger arrive.

'Sorry we're late,' Iris says. 'Just as we were leaving my mother called... long distance... all the way from Miami. I just couldn't get her off.' She hunches her shoulders in apology.

'That's okay,' Rosie says.

'Yeah,' Joe agrees.

'Yeah,' Rosie again. 'We got plentya time.'

Iris is short, wears a denim skirt made from a pair of jeans, Dr. Scholl's sandals and a black leotard top. Her breasts are large for such a small person. Joe figures they would probably hang a lot lower if she were wearing a loose blouse. Roger is about Joe's height, a little stockier and black. Joe's angry at Rosie for not telling him this beforehand. He doesn't think of himself as a racist. He's been through public schools and the army and works with black people every day. But when he's in a social situation, like this one, he's always afraid he'll say something wrong.

'Roger, you know Rosie... and this is her husband, Joe.'

'Hya.' They shake hands. *What else'd I be doin here if I wasn't her fuckin husband?*

For most of dinner Iris and Rosie do most of the talking and mostly to each other. Gradually Joe becomes fairly comfortable with Roger. He listens and Roger talks. Talkative people usually bore the hell out of Joe, and if he isn't interested in someone he rarely goes out of his way to appear so. He usually responds in bored monosyllables until the talker gives up. But in this case, being confined to a table with a black man and a stranger at that, Joe feels obliged to appear interested and is surprised to find out that Roger has something to say. Roger's an architecture major at Cooper Union and plans to go into urban design. He tells Joe that he wants to design public housing projects that are fit for people to live in.

'You know what I'm saying?'

'Yeah.' Joe smiles at Roger. 'Sounds like a good idea.'

'You see, most public housing deprives people of any sense of individuality, comfort or independence...' Roger pauses, liking the sound of his own voice. 'The steel and concrete halls and the boxes they call apartment buildings are really jails to imprison the poor by constantly reminding them that they are wards of the state.'

'I see what ya mean. Ya can start right here in this neighborhood. Tear it down an put up nice houses like they got out in Queens. Tear it all the fuck down. Yeah. Ya gotta good idea there, Roger.'

'Something like that,' Roger agrees, looking at Joe like he might be a little crazy.

Joe notices the look in Roger's eye and decides that next time maybe he won't understand so well. He mentions that he works for Brooklyn/Queens Water Resources but doesn't mention his job. Before Roger gave him that look, which really pissed him off, Joe felt that Roger represented a little of what he *might have been* had he stayed in school. And what he might be is something Joe rarely thinks about. He decides that Roger is simply a snob like his friend Iris. *A black snob.* He wishes Rosie had told him.

* * *

The theater is filled. They get to their seats as the title credits are showing.

THE PASSENGER
A MICHELANGELO ANTONIONI FILM
STARRING
JACK NICHOLSON AND MARIA SCHNEIDER

'Joe,' Rosie whispers, poking him, 'you remember Maria Schneider. She's the one from *Last Tango*.' Another film she managed to wrestle Joe into seeing.

Joe sits upright, making sure he can see over the head of the guy in front of him. Boy, does he remember Maria Schneider.

Everyone but Joe becomes engrossed in the film. He can't figure out what's going on. All he knows is that Jack Nicholson and Maria Schneider are running from something and he can't figure out what it is. One scene grabs his attention and keeps him preoccupied for the rest of the film. The scene is of an execution somewhere in Africa. It happens suddenly and seems to have nothing to do with the rest of the film. Joe can't figure out what the guy is supposed to be guilty of. He's tied to an oil drum and not blindfolded. He has no expression on his face whatsoever. The firing squad doesn't shoot all at once like you'd expect, but one at a time. Joe once saw an ARVN patrol execute four men suspected of being Cong. They were lined up along a road outside Khe Sanh, soldiers on one side, prisoners on the other. There was no command to fire. They fired when they chose to, as often as they chose to, and at whichever of the four men they felt, for whatever reason, it was their duty to execute. That was the first time Joe heard the *pthunk* a bullet makes as it rips into flesh. Now, sitting in a movie theatre, in July, in New York, he's hearing the same sound or a damn good imitation of it. The man shudders with each shot but still registers no expression. After the third *pthunk* his head spills over onto his choot. After the fourth his body hangs, a bloody sack, from the oil drum his wrists are tied to.

Joe nudges Rosie. 'Jesus, could that be real?'

'SSSH, probably not.'

Rosie, Iris and Roger like the movie. So do all the people on the double line passing up the aisle and out into the lobby. A couple steps out of the next row separating Joe from Rosie, Iris and Roger, who are too busy talking about the movie to notice. Joe's glad about the human barrier coming between himself and the rest of the party because he didn't like the film and doesn't feel like talking about it. He knows it meant something to them, something he has no access to and no interest in. He walks slower and lets the distance increase. A woman in front of him tells her date that she thinks Antonioni is a genius. She also tells him that even though she spent a week's salary doing it, she spent the Fourth of July weekend in Martha's Vineyard with her friend Beverly from work.

He sees the trio before they see him. They're standing under the marquee. Rosie's on tiptoe trying to find him in the crowd. He can see she's angry.

'What happened?'

'Got cut off.'

'You should walk faster.'

'What for?'

Iris cuts in. 'Hey, you guys want to come over? We got some grass and a half-gallon of wine and it's not that late.'

'Sure.' Rosie's for it.

Joe'd rather go home, but it would be impossible to do that and still avoid a fight with Rosie. He agreed to come to the movie. He has to stick it out. As they walk south along Second Avenue, Joe wonders how Rosie can get mad at him for something as stupid as walking slow. He didn't want to go to the fuckin movie anyway.

Rosie wonders why Joe never realizes what an obstinate
son of a bitch he can be without even trying.

Iris lives in a two-room apartment on East Fifth Street.
The painted wooden floors are on a slant and the bathtub is
in the kitchen. There's a fireplace, varnished brick walls,
hanging plants all over the place, gates on the windows and
a police lock, with a long iron bar, that intrudes three feet
into the kitchen. Rosie admires the brick walls and a tall
avocado plant that stands next to a radiator which Iris, for
no other reason than wanting to, had painted yellow. Joe
wonders why anyone who didn't have to would live in a
neighborhood where they had to have bars on their
windows. He wonders if Roger thinks this is better than
public housing.

Everyone's sitting in a circle on the floor. Roger lights a
joint and passes it to Joe. Joe can count on one hand the
times he's smoked dope since he was in the service. He
knows, in a situation like this, that it could make him
uptight, so he fills a glass with wine, takes a deep drag and
passes the joint to Rosie.

'Did you like the movie?' Roger asks him.

'It was okay.'

'I really dug it,' Roger says, gasping smoke. 'I especially
liked the concept of being a passenger in another man's
life.'

'Yeah,' Joe accepting the joint.

'And that shot at the end. Seven minutes without cutting
away. It was like a living painting.'

'Yeah, it was okay.'

Roger gets up to put on a record. 'Hey, any requests?'

'Yeah,' Iris says. 'Laura Nyro.'

'You've been listening to her all day. How about Miles
Davis? You guys like jazz?'

'Fine with me.'

'Yeah, whatever... '

'I'd rather hear Laura Nyro.'

'You're outvoted.' Roger sits down, lights another joint and passes it to Joe. That's that. Then looks at Joe, high and ready to talk. Joe'd rather be on the moon.

Joe asks him if he thought the execution scene was real, but Roger doesn't remember it. This surprises Joe since it's the only scene he remembers clearly. He can't recall half the stuff Roger was talking about.

'Ya know. Where they got that colored guy tied to an oil drum and they shoot em one at a time.'

'Colored,' Roger repeats, laughing. 'We's cawled black folks nowadays.'

A wave of paranoia suddenly crashes over Joe. He feels the kind of embarrassment he sometimes feels just being with Joe Flushing Avenue when he says things like 'your people' to the black guys at work, only worse. He's also angry. *That self-righteous son of a bitch. I shoulda said nigger.*

'Sorry Roger,' hating saying it. 'I always thought the word "black" was like the word "Jew." A guy on the six o'clock news can say it, but when you say it to somebody's face it's an insult.'

'It's not. I can say "white," can't I?'

'Yeah.'

That wiseass college scumbag really thinks he scored a point.

Joe finishes his glass of wine, lies back with his hands behind his head and stares at the ceiling. *Scumbag.* He keeps staring until Roger finds someone else to talk to.

Roger gets up, flips the record and sits down facing Iris, who's telling a joke. Something about a cannoli that's filled with spermicide. Everyone thinks it's funny. Joe lies there, hating Miles Davis, avocado plants and that dumb fuckin yellow radiator.

Rosie sleeps for the whole subway ride, which is okay
with Joe. He figures anything he'd have to say to her right
now would only cause a fight. He watches their reflection
in the dark window across from them, he sitting up, his head
framed by a Salem ad, and Rosie, asleep against his
shoulder. He imagines he's driving somewhere in a car
with Maria Schneider. They pull up to a hotel and a
porter, in livery, carries their bags. As soon as they're alone
in their room, he lifts her off the floor, like Marlon Brando
in *Last Tango*, and lets her have it standing up.

6

JOE'S STANDING at the base of an eight-by-fifteen rectangle of shade thrown onto the sidewalk by the aluminium awning in front of the Q & T Diner on Atlantic Avenue. The hoods of the new Buicks shine on Victor's-Queens-Buick lot on 113th Street. Older cars hold and spread the sunlight in dust and flat paint in Victor's used-car annex across Atlantic Avenue.

Standing at the end of the shadow nearest the curb is Mr. Dugan, who, until about fifteen years ago, owned a grocery store on the corner of 109th Street where Joe and his friends used to hang out on summer afternoons sucking ice cubes from the soda box. Sometimes he'd let Joe put on an apron and help him sort out the coupons that mothers would cut out of newspapers. They've passed each other hundreds of times in the neighborhood without exchanging a word. He knew Joe as a kid but not as an adult. The store that housed Dugan's Grocery has since done a five-year stint as a sign painter's shop and is now TWO

BROTHERS ALUMINUM SIDING COMPANY. Mr. Dugan's
standing on the curb, his hands in his pockets, whistling
with vibrato and jiggling his change.

It's about 9:30. Rosie'll probably sleep till noon. Joe
woke up about 8:00, then after lying in bed for a halfhour,
walked over to the Q & T for coffee. He doesn't sleep well
and never has. He can't remember a night, excluding those
when he's had a few beers, when he simply closed his eyes
and fell asleep. When Joe was a kid he thought of sleep as
an enemy, something everyone else could do because they
were told they had to and believed it. He particularly
dreaded naptime. He remembers playing under the
kitchen table with his cousin Al while his mother and his
aunt Anne would sit, drinking coffee and talking. He and
Al were looking up his aunt's dress as far as a thin
shadowed line, about halfway between her knees and hips,
where her soft thighs pressed together. Then, without any
warning, an alarm would go off in the two mothers' heads
announcing naptime, and they'd scoop up Joe and Al, haul
them off to the bedroom where his parents slept and dump
them on the big double bed.

Al could fall asleep with as much effort as it took to close
his eyes and wait sixty seconds. Joe hated him for sleeping
so easily and for not feeling as pissed as he was at being
dragged away from their imaginary journey further up
Aunt Anne's dress, and for believing them when they told
him that he actually *needed* to sleep in the middle of the day.
Joe'd watch his fat little Kool-Aid-red lips press in and out,
then he'd lie back and stare at the baby pictures hanging
on the wall opposite the bed. There was one of Joe, one of
his brother, James, and, in between, there was a big one of
the two of them sitting on a horse. They were wearing
cowboy hats and were held on by a man with a big
moustache who was also wearing a cowboy hat, only
bigger. In the picture Joe was crying. He remembers

staring at that picture and wondering how it got taken because he didn't know the man with the moustache and he couldn't remember ever having seen a real horse in his life.

A group of teenage girls in cutoff jeans, T-shirts with the bikini straps showing at the tops, a blanket and a portable radio pass through the patch of shade between Joe and Mr. Dugan on their way to the Rockaway-bound el train on Liberty Avenue. Then two cops, a rare sight on Atlantic Avenue, especially on foot, pass heading east towards Jamaica. As they stroll by, not noticing either Mr. Dugan or Joe, he feels a mild sense of comfort, of relief, that he's not an outlaw. This feeling of pleasure at watching two cops walk by and knowing that in their course of duty they won't be chasing you, but some other poor son of a bitch, is probably, Joe figures, what keeps people, even after working twenty years as a fucking meter reader, from robbing banks or blowing up the White House. After they pass, the feeling turns around. He senses, in not noticing him, they robbed him of a chance to feel he is someone who might have some kind of effect on the world, criminal or otherwise. *Fuck em.* They just walked past someone capable of sitting on top of a sky-scraper with a monster howitzer and blowing New York to bits. A trained artillery specialist who can make a hole in the ground out of a squad car from eleven miles away, and they pass him, paying him no more notice than the parked cars or old Mr. Dugan, standing on the curb, jiggling his change.

The traffic has thickened. Cars filled with families pass on their way to Grandma's, church, Rockaway, Coney Island or even Bear Mountain. 'If ya stay at an even thirty,' Joe's father used to say, 'ya can make every light on Atlantic from Jamaica ta Brooklyn.'

Joe runs down the list of options he made for a shrink at the Veterans' Hospital nearly five years ago — escape routes he might consider if things got really bad.

Three months after his discharge he still hadn't found a job. He remembered one of the leaflets given him along with his discharge that said if he ever had a problem the door to the counseling office at the VA Hospital was always open.

Dr. Seidman, who told Joe to call him Bob, explained that this meant psychiatric counseling, not job counselling, but as long as he was there, why don't they just talk. He said he couldn't help in the employment area but he had a suggestion for Joe. To make a list of, say, five options — jobs he'd like to apply for, places he'd like to see, changes he might want to make in his life if he became unhappy — really unhappy — with the way things are now. Go on, take a pencil, do it right now, he told Joe, who thought to himself that one problem he didn't have was the inability to recognize an asshole when he saw one.

Joe crumpled it up and threw it out before he reached the elevator, but the list stuck in his head. Sometimes he runs it back to himself to pass the time, like when he's driving out to a sector, or when he's standing around, like now.

1. Reenlist (Then I'd really need a shrink).
2. Go back to college (let my wife support me — you don't get shit from the GI Bill — sit in a classroom filled with eighteen-year-old assholes).
3. Knock up Rosie (only she don't want to — she said to wait).
4. Get fat like Joe Flushing

Avenue and stop wanting to
knock up Rosie (which he said
marriage is all about — even
though he ain't ever been
married).

5. Take my half of our savings
   (about $600), go to California
   and hang out with Otis
   Redding, which is what Vern
   who was in my Field Arty
   company said he was going to
   do.

Soon afterwards, Joe's father called and told him that
someone he knew said they were hiring at Brooklyn/
Queens Water Resources.

He wonders, standing there, what Bob meant by *really
unhappy*. How do you know when you're not just ordinarily
unhappy? Maybe a buzzer goes off when you get there.
Maybe you do more than just imagine blowing something
up.

Joe recognizes Denise, the cashier at the A & P, as soon
as he sees her, walking towards him a block away. She's
wearing a T-shirt with a picture of a whale across the chest,
jeans and white track sneakers. She looks good. When Joe
looked down her blouse the other night, he knew what he
was looking for, but the small pale cones he found inside
her gray cashier's smock really threw him for a loop. It was
their vulnerability, hanging there, in that one private
moment in the middle of a busy supermarket. They made
her seem so different, a woman, so unlike him. They existed
in total contrast to the dull, indifferent cashier's gaze that

protected her. It's a look he's seen a thousand times on the faces of women behind cash registers and counters. He reads it as a constant response to the shit work and particularly to any guy who might come on to her, letting him know that if he's going to be as full of shit as the next guy, she'd rather not hear it.

Which is why she surprises the hell out of Joe by smiling, curious as to how he knows her name, when he says hi.

'Do I know you?'

'Yeah... well, not really. I was by the A & P the other night.'

'Are you the guy who was buying baby food?'

'Uh uh. That couldna been me.'

She laughs. 'I ring up a hundred sales a day. It's hard to remember.'

'Yeah. Where ya going? The beach?'

'Nah.'

'I figured ya mighta been. I seen at least twenny people with towels an stuff. Good day for it.'

'It sure is. But I have to go to work.'

'On Sunday? Jeez, what a drag.' Joe's still amazed at her friendliness. She's not an old hag like Taxi. She could meet all the guys she wants without having to stop in front of a diner and have a conversation with a guy she doesn't know from Adam.

'Hey. I just remembered. I gotta pick up some cornflakes. Why don't I walk with ya.'

'Sure.'

The surprises keep coming.

'Hey. How come it says, "Help Save the Whales" on your T-shirt?'

'Because we're killing them. All over the world they're killing whales and there's not many left. This T-shirt cost five dollars and the money went to the Help Save the Whales Fund.'

'How many are left?'

'I don't know. Not many.'

'Jeez. That's a shame.'

In the time it takes to walk five blocks Joe's told her his name, age, nationality, occupation, and that if he knew where to get one, he'd buy a whale T-shirt too. Denise is an English major at Queens College and only works part-time at the A & P. She lives with her family but wants to move out. She also writes poems.

'Yeah? Ya got any with ya?'

'No,' laughing. 'I don't bring poems to work.'

'Too bad. Hey, maybe you'll show me one sometime.'

Joe's been waiting for an in, some situation he could set up that would entail seeing her again.

'May-be,' she says.

Joe wonders what it means when you accent it that way. *May*-be.

They walk down Lefferts Boulevard, approaching the A & P. Its brick walls and ad-covered windows grow larger by the second. Joe knows it's his last chance to say something that will definitely establish a future meeting.

'Hey, why don't ya play hookey and we'll cut out ta Rockaway.'

'You're crazy!'

'C'mon. C'mon.'

'I'd love to,' frowning and smiling at the same time like she might actually go for it, 'but I can't.'

He knew she probably wouldn't. But he also knew that the crazy suggestion would please her and quickly close some of the distance between them.

'Look. Why don't I come by some night after work an we can go for a walk or somethin. An maybe you'll even read me some of your poems.'

'I don't know... I guess.'

'Sure, why not.'
'Yeah... why not.'

Rosie expected to wake up to an hour of bitching about
how lousy the film was and what an asshole Roger is.
Instead, Joe had made her breakfast and was sitting in
front of the TV, oddly contented, eating a bowl of cornflakes. He was watching the Sunday Morning Movie, *Hold
That Ghost*, starring Abbott and Costello.

After breakfast Rosie decides to go out into the yard and
sunbathe. She puts on a red and blue two-piece and walks
out into the living room, walking between Joe and the TV,
modeling for him. His eyes are glued to the set.

'Why don't ya get some sun, Joe? Weekends are too short
to spend them watching TV.'

'Nah.' Lou Costello is standing on a chair, reaching up
the throat of a stuffed moose head, pulling out thousands of
dollars in paper money. 'What a tonsil!' he says, pulling
out a roll the size of his fist, while Bud Abbott and Joan
Davis scurry frantically in the shower of bills, trying to
catch as many as they can. 'It's almost over. I think I'll go
out for a walk.'

Joe first walks back to the A & P. He stands out front,
half hidden by a Sanka ad, and looks inside. Denise is at her
register. He watches her pack a shopping bag. First, she
puts one bag inside another. Then packs them, canned
goods on the bottom, then vegetables, cereal and various
other things on top. Finally she drops the receipt on top
and hands the bag to a woman who probably just came
from Mass because she's still wearing a small white lace
handkerchief bobby-pinned to her hair. Joe doesn't hang
around. If she sees him she might think he's too interested.

He walks over to Mary's, stops out front and looks in the
open door. The first thing he sees is Joe Flushing Avenue's

wide back. Two bands of sweat start at his shoulders, soak down the rounded back of his shirt and come together at his lower back. Mary's probably in the kitchen. Joe Flushing Avenue's holding his head up with his hands, his elbows propped against the bar. The TV is on with the sound turned off and a stand-up fan is blowing hot air against his back. Joe wonders how he could get so smashed this early in the day. It's probably still last night for him. 'Knock Three Times' is playing on the jukebox. Joe Flushing Avenue is rocking his barstool and humming along with Tony Orlando about a phrase behind. Joe pauses a moment before walking out onto Atlantic Avenue, to watch a cougar, on the silent TV, leap off a Lincoln-Mercury sign and change into a beautiful woman as it lands on the shining hood of a new car.

7

WAKING to heat is slow.

Rosie's afraid to let herself fall asleep with the air conditioner on. She's afraid of electricity, dangerous, hot juice that courses through wires hidden in the walls of the apartment with the power to glow in light bulbs and cause the air conditioner to hum and make cool air out of hot air. By day she could care less. But at night, while lying in the dark, such mysterious things rear their persistent heads.

A dream of Diane Salerno, who he went out with in his senior year of high school, slowly pulling off her T-shirt in the back seat of his parents' '64 Chevy, reluctantly evaporates from Joe's waking mind as he realizes that the aggravating electric buzz is the alarm clock and the hand wrapped around his semi-hard penis is his own.

He can't reconcile waking up to a hot summer day and having to go to work on it. For more than half of his twenty-seven summers, such mornings preceded the beach, TV, stoop sitting, working out in the gym at the boys' club, or at

worst, a part time job as a delivery boy for D'Aurio's Meat
Market. He unhappily begins to realize that he is someone
who is going to get up, have coffee, punch in, drive out to a
strange neighborhood, go down into its basements with its
rats and roaches and read its water meters until each of the
names on his sector cards has little numbers written in the
blank spaces next to it. When all of the spaces have
numbers in them, he has, according to Brooklyn/Queens
Water Resources, fulfilled his part of a contract. He has
earned his $40.55 before taxes and can go home, a
functioning citizen.

'Shit. Maybe I'll call in sick.' He nudges Rosie, who
doesn't have to get up for another hour.

' Ya can't. Ya called in last Monday.'

'Yeah, but I *was* sick.'

'You had a hangover.'

'That's sick, ain't it?'

'It don't matter. Ya can't call in sick twice in two weeks.'

'Shit.'

Joe tries to pull apart two glasses that have gotten stuck,
one inside the other, then decides, fuck it, he'll skip the
orange juice this morning and drops them back onto the
drainboard. He pours a mug of coffee and sets it down on
an open *New York Post* Rosie left sitting on the kitchen table
the night before. He reads a headline:

RAILROAD SUICIDE REPLAYED BOYFRIEND'S DEATH

At first he's just a little bemused, a little interested. Most
things he reads in newspapers are, to him, only half real
because they rarely occur where he can see them. He reads
on:

> Precisely at 5:15 P.M. Lorraine Scheele opened
> wide her arms as if to welcome death and waited
> on the Long Island Railroad tracks for the same

train that had killed her boyfriend the week
before.

Caught in the replay of a nightmare, unable to
brake in time, the same engineer desperately
blasted his horn.

Lorraine Scheele, 22, a slim figure in blue jeans
and a white shirt, cupped her hands over her ears
as the train hit, killing her instantly. 'They were
very close,' her grieving mother said yesterday.
'We really don't know what happened. She
seemed to be a happy girl. She had a lot to live
for.'

'That poor bastard,' Joe says aloud. 'Hitting two people
in one week. I hope he gets a vacation. Jesus. She musta
been nuts. Poor fuckin bastard...'

'What?' Rosie asks from the bedroom.

'Nothin.'

The article somehow caps off one hell of a crazy weekend for Joe. First Sammy's El and Florence, then the film
and that asshole, Roger, and Denise in the *Help Save the
Whales* T-shirt. For no reason Joe can figure, a parade of
the things that happened to him in the last sixty hours
begins to pass through his mind. At one end is an ear of
yellow and white New Jersey corn. At the other is a photo
of Lorraine Scheele's plain American face in rimless
hexagonal glasses that the *New York Post* borrowed from
her high school yearbook. Suddenly it's like watching a
movie. The parade grows. Hundreds of things have been
waiting in his mind for the event. A fat Hell's Angel in a
coonskin cap, a Cong being shot in the chest, a boy
squatting like Son of Sam about to fire, a yellow radiator,
Maria Schneider looking back from a moving car, a child's
sneaker, a dead tortoise, a Reddi Wip can.

He wishes these things were going through someone
else's head. He knows they all have something to do with
each other. And that *something* is the reason they happened

in the first place. If he could see them all at once, clearly, maybe he could figure out what it is. Then maybe he could understand what it is that conjures the image of Lou Costello pulling money from a moose's mouth when in the first place he's trying to recall Denise's small pale breasts. *It's a fuckin brick wall.* All these things posing before his eyes as if they had minds of their own. *A brick wall.* If he could see how each one ends and the one next to it, or over it, or under it, begins. You can't see all the bricks in a brick wall. You can see the wall, the bricks vague and blended. But when you try to see all the bricks your focus changes, and you have to look at them one at a time.

Joe and Joe Flushing Avenue are driving out to Corona. It's 9:25 and hotter. They like reading meters in Corona because it's a safe neighborhood, and like Richmond Hill, and unlike most neighborhoods that are richer or poorer, the people respect someone wearing a uniform. Or half a uniform, which is what Joe's wearing. He's got on his green Water Resources shirt with sneakers and jeans held up by a frayed, fifteen-year-old Boy Scout belt.

Joe Flushing Avenue is at the wheel. At a light he reaches into his shirt pocket, pulls out a button and flips it, like a coin, to Joe.

'What's this?'

'A button.'

'Yeah, but what do I do with it?'

'Ya shove it up Jimmy Carter's ass. It keeps the peanuts from comin out.'

Joe looks out the window wondering how Joe Flushing Avenue manages to go through life without ever realizing what an asshole he is. He looks down a side street and sees what he at first thinks is two dogs fucking but turns out to be a young boy, kneeling and writing on the pavement with chalk.

'I got it from Florence. She said to give it ta ya.'

'You're shittin me.'

'It musta been right after ya left. She comes inta the bedroom and there's me and Taxi humpin away an says, look, if you two are gonna have a goddam marathon then you can do it someplace else. Boy, she was pissed. Why'd ya leave anyway?'

'I just had ta split.'

'I know the feeling. Only I wish you'da told me.'

Queens Boulevard is clogged with Manhattan-bound traffic. They decide to turn off and wind toward Corona via side streets. Joe stares, dumbfounded, at the button.

'Anyway, we're leavin an I see she's got tears in her eyes, so I say, what's up? and she says, nothin.'

Joe wishes they'd get there. When Joe Flushing Avenue knows he's got his attention, he enjoys it and drags each sentence out with ten minutes of bullshit.

'Get ta the point.'

'I am, I am. So she says, there's nothin wrong, so I head for the door but she stops me an hands me this button. It musta come off when the two a ya were fuckin. So she says, give it ta Joe. Maybe he'll come ta Sammy's some night an give it back.'

Joe doesn't answer.

'Ya ever goin back?'

'Nah.'

'Then why don't ya give it to me. I'll give it back. *And how.*'

'Nah.'

'Why not? You're not gonna use it.'

Suddenly the button has become the currency with which Joe Flushing Avenue can buy a fuck. Joe flips it out the window.

'Hey, what dja do that for? Why didn't ya give it ta me?'

'Because she'd probably tella ya ta keep it.'

* * *

After an otherwise uneventful Monday in Corona, they're sitting around a big table at the office waiting to punch out. There are six or seven empty takeout cups sitting on the table and a white bakery box, also empty except for some crumbs and wax paper. The box has no top because that morning Lenny Breger, one of the readers, tore it off to write down the names of the horses running in the fourth race at Aqueduct. Joe Flushing Avenue lights a cigarette, blows out the match in the first exhaled smoke and drops it into the bakery box.

Joe gets up, goes over to the punch clock and watches the minute hand creep through the last, few, protracted minutes before five o'clock.

8

CAPTAIN CAVANAUGH is bagging groceries as Denise rings them up. Cavanaugh, who is mentally retarded, was dubbed 'Captain' by the kids in the neighborhood because he used to spend his days hanging around the firehouse on Jamaica Avenue. When an alarm came in he'd jump on his bicycle and race after the trucks. Then he'd try to help the firemen by directing traffic or yelling at kids to keep out of the way. Sometimes he'd just pace back and forth with the authoritative air of a man with a reason for being there.

Once there was a fire in one of the big apartment buildings on Park Lane South. Joe and some friends who'd been playing basketball in the park stopped to watch the commotion. Cavanaugh had been relieved of traffic duty by a real fireman and was marching angrily up and down the sidewalk shooing kids off one of the fire trucks. There were about two dozen firemen scattered up the fire escape, leading up a hose. Cavanaugh looked up, saw them and stopped. Then, seized with inspiration, he put his hand to his forehead and shouted to the firemen, 'COME DOWN IN ALPHABETICAL ORDER.'

Joe figures that he's probably about thirty-five, though it's hard to tell for sure. His large, never-corrected overbite has caused his face to remain a child's face until now, when, having managed to skip young adulthood, he is passing directly into middle age. Joe is watching him, on that cusp between childhood and middle age, gently wedging a dozen eggs into a bed he's made for them between a loaf of white bread and a roll of paper towels.

There's a woman with a full cart and a man with a six-pack of Schaefer half-quarts still to go before Joe gets to Denise. It's Wednesday, 6:45. Joe told Rosie he might be going out to Aqueduct with some guys after work.

Denise hasn't seen him yet because she never looks up. She looks at the prices on the groceries as she pushes them down the counter to Cavanaugh, and at her fingers pressing the cash-register keys.

She's surprised to see him, standing there, groceryless and smiling. Joe wonders if she might not be all that happy about him showing up.

'Hi.'

'Hi.' Denise smiles.

'Hi,' Cavanaugh adds, wondering how Joe is and why he's standing there without any groceries.

Joe, reaching for something to say, motions to the woman behind him to go ahead and steps back.

'Listen,' he says to Denise, who is ringing up a chicken. 'I got a great idea. We'll have dinner. Anything ya want in the whole supermarket. We can eat in the park.'

The woman pays and Cavanaugh sets her bag into her shopping cart.

Denise looks at Joe. 'Are you married?'

The question surprises the shit out of him. He expected a

simple yes or no. He just stares at her. Then looks over at Cavanaugh, who also wants to know.

'You are, aren't you?'

'Uh huh.' He's sure this has finished it.

'It's okay. I just like to know the truth. You better hurry. I get off in ten minutes. Get some cheese and bread and bring it here. Then maybe you'll run over to the liquor store for a bottle of wine.'

'Sure.' He wanders over to the dairy case, confused as to what has just happened. He looks back and sees Cavanaugh smiling at him.

They're walking up Lefferts Boulevard toward Atlantic, backtracking the steps they took on Sunday when he walked her to work. It's a clear, hot evening. Joe's wearing his green work shirt with the sleeves rolled up and the three top buttons opened, exposing the thin silver chain of the St. Christopher medal he's worn since his confirmation. He asks Denise why his being married doesn't bother her.

'Marriage is outdated. If marriage served all our needs would you be standing in front of a diner all by yourself on a Sunday morning asking girls you don't know if you can walk them to work?'

'Yeah, I guess you're right.' Joe doesn't know if he agrees or not. Marriage hasn't brought him much happiness but he can't figure out any alternatives. What he does know is that Denise pronounces her words much more properly than most people he knows. If she wants to play it her way, that's all right with him.

She prefers to eat in the park on 106th Street because she'll have less of a walk home afterwards. Joe isn't all that pleased with the idea because the route takes them right past his corner and if Rosie just happened to see them, the shit would hit the fan.

'Big deal. So she sees you. You're just walking down the

street with someone you know from the neighborhood. Don't be so uptight.'

'Okay.' What she doesn't know is that Rosie sees things differently. She'd break whatever was nearest and hardest over his head and ask questions later. But so far Denise is calling the shots. It's her ball game.

The big mercury lamps are already on but shed no light in the bright, treeless playground dusk. The park is divided by fences into two main sections. You enter into an area with swings, a sandbox, monkey bars, seesaws and painted hopscotch courts. There's a row of benches filled with teenagers pressed tightly against each other. Mostly they're in couples, each turned with their backs against the others, making out or talking. Along their feet, running the length of the benches, is a three-foot-wide strip of cigarette butts, candy wrappers, broken glass and beer cans that looks as if it had been left there by a receding tide.

The other half of the park is divided into softball courts, basketball courts and, at the far end, four concrete-wall handball courts. Over ten years ago some kids ripped away a section of hurricane fence behind the basketball courts and made an unofficial entrance that saved them a walk around the block. Except for two kids playing one-on-one basketball the whole section is empty.

Joe and Denise head for the handball courts, which are closed in and quiet. She pulls a portable radio from her shoulder bag, and they begin to lay out their supper on folded paper bags and wax paper. There's Swiss cheese and Italian bread as well as a jar of stuffed olives and a bag of Chips Ahoy! cookies Denise had added to their provisions while Joe was getting wine. She pulls out a package of twenty-four paper cups and laughs.

'This is the smallest I could get.'

'Great. We'll drink each round out of a new cup.' Joe

had bought a half-gallon, hoping she knew how to drink.

'So how's meter reading?' She breaks off a piece of cheese.

'A drag. Today I was workin out in South Jamaica. This super shows me the door ta the basement an when I open it I see this Doberman pinscher headin up the stairs with my ass in mind. I slammed it just as he got ta the top.'

It hadn't happened today. It actually happened two months ago but he wanted to tell her something interesting.

'Jesus. What'd you do?'

'I turn around an that dumb fuckin super's just standin there smilin. I'da nailed em but ya can get in trouble for that, besides, ya can never tell who he's got waitin ta come outta the woodwork.'

'Why don't you quit?'

'An do what?'

'Why not go back to school?'

'You gonna pay my rent?'

The sun is setting behind the Greek Orthodox church across Atlantic Avenue, and the light from the mercury lamps becomes more defined against the clear, darkening sky. Joe pulls two more cups from the package and pours another round.

'Hey, didja bring any poems with ya?' Joe changes the subject. He feels more in control when he's doing the asking and she's doing the answering. He can stay clear of himself.

'No. I told you I don't bring my poems to work.'

'Don't ya know any of em by heart?'

'Well, there's one I just finished yesterday... but why would you want to hear it anyway?'

'I don't know. Why do ya write poems if ya not gonna let anybody see em?'

'I just don't know how you'll respond. Maybe you'll

laugh. Maybe you won't understand.'

'Try me.'

'Okay.' She turns the radio down.

Joe leans his face towards hers. She smiles and pushes him back, then says, no, she won't do it if he's going to stare right at her.

'Okay. I won't.' He leans back against the wall.

She concentrates a moment the way Joe remembers concentrating when he was on the high school gymnastics team and was about to do a routine.

'Okay. It's called "The Hunter Meets a Flower in a Dream."' She looks over at Joe to see if he has any comments on the title, then begins.

> I dreamt I was a wild flower
> standing alone
> in the corner of a field.
> The sun was setting
> and my petals felt warm...

'Are you listening?'

'Yeah. It's great. Go on.'

> And a hunter
> who was also dreaming
> was passing my way and discovered me.
> He bent over
> and pressed his nose into me.
> In that moment
> when man met flower
> he possessed all my beauty.
> Then, passed on his way,
> carrying me forever with him.

Well... ' She gulps down her wine. 'What did you think?'

There's a single tear in her eye, partly from embarrassment, and partly because her own poem had moved her.

Joe doesn't respond to the poem. He responds to the tear.

'Jesus, Denise. It was beautiful.' He smiles and pours more wine.

'Do you really think so, Joe?'

'Yeah. I mean it.'

She leans forward, throws her arms around Joe's neck and kisses him. He resists for a moment in surprise, but when she opens his mouth with her tongue, he immediately comes to terms with the situation. They kiss for a long time. While they're kissing, the basketball players go home and the sun sets without them.

Joe's feeling great and, to his own surprise, thanks her.

'Why?' Denise asks.

'I don't know. I feel calm... not thinkin... just bein here... it's nice.'

'Wow.' Denise looks up to find they're the only ones left in the park. 'I'm getting drunk.'

'Me too.'

'So let's have another.' She throws the empty cup against the wall as if she were throwing a stem glass into a fire.

Joe wants to open up to her. He hasn't wanted to open up to another person since he first met Rosie. He feels Denise will welcome him. He wants to turn on the lights under which she can see him.

'Denise, I wanna tell ya somethin. I don't know how you're gonna respond but I'm gonna tell ya anyway.'

'Okay. Tell me.'

'Well, when you were ringin up my stuff I looked down your blouse and, Jesus, Denise, you're beautiful.' He can't believe he just sat there and told a girl he hardly knows that he once looked down her blouse.

She throws her arms around him again.

'Joe, it's you. You're the hunter in the poem. I was writing about you and didn't even know it.'

'Yeah, I guess so.' For the first time Joe actually understands what the poem is about, but he's not sure if he's got anything in common with this hunter, or if he'd want to. It all seems a little silly but that's okay. He's feeling fine.

They sit facing each other, Joe with his legs crossed, Denise with hers over his knees and dangling behind him. He watches her face. She's telling him about her creative writing teacher who just published a book of stories, one of which is about a man who receives a package of human wrists in the mail.

'Yech. What does he do?'

'He goes on a trip to find the guy who sent it.'

'Shit. That's what I'd do. Does he find him?'

'No. He can't even find the guy's town.'

'Why not?'

'Cause it's not on any map.'

'What a dumb story.'

Before Joe realizes that it's the failing mercury lamps that are causing the play of light and shadow on Denise's face, it's pitch black. Not a light anywhere. Nothing. Joe walks over to the fence and sees that the only sources of light, for as far as the eye can see, are the headlights of the cars on Atlantic Avenue. They form a bright band, white on one side, red on the other, that stretches all the way into the pitch-black horizon.

'Jesus Christ. What the fuck happened?' He stumbles back to Denise. 'Turn up the radio.'

The announcer is telling people not to drive if possible, to stay where they are. 'I repeat. There has been a power failure. Spokesmen for Con Ed report that there is no power in all of New York's five boroughs and in parts of Long Island, Connecticut and New Jersey as well. As of this time we have received no word as to when the power will be restored.'

Joe lights a match and finds the spot he had been sitting in.

'This is fuckin crazy!'

'I think it's great,' Denise answers, finding a seat next to Joe against the wall.

'I think *you're* fuckin crazy too.' He drops an arm around her shoulder.

They can see flashlights now, and candles, moving through the black on Ninety-fourth Avenue. There are no stars, but you can see the outlines of roofs poking into the dark milky-lavender sky.

'I think it's great,' Denise repeats. 'It's like being the only people in the whole world.'

Joe slips his right hand under her T-shirt, lifting it slowly, finding her breasts.

'I've wanted to do this ever since that night in the A & P. Now that we're the last two people on earth I guess it's okay.'

He pulls up her T-shirt until it gathers in a roll at her neck. She reaches behind her, crossing her arms to pull it off, then spreads it out on the concrete, what little bed they'll have, and lies back on it. The skin on her forehead gives off a pale glow in the blanket of shadow that covers the handball court. She lifts herself toward him and pulls his face to her breasts. The headlights of a car pulling out of a driveway on Ninety-fourth Avenue scrape the wall over them without a sound. Joe is lifting her pants out from under her raised hips and she is fumbling with his belt, then his fly. Her hand makes room for itself and slides all the way under his ass, then strokes upward, slowly. Joe groans with his lips glued to her nipple.

'I want to get completely undressed,' she whispers, and they do. In the middle of the public night; socks, shoes, everything. The concrete smells of chalk and sneakers.

They fuck slow and easy. They're the only two people in the whole world and have all the time in it.

Denise is lying on her side with her leg over Joe's hip and her head on his shoulder. He can feel his come becoming crusty on the inside of her thigh. A Marlboro glows in his right hand.

The radio brings the rest of the world uncomfortably near:

'Off-duty police have been called in to help control the looting in the city's high-crime areas. Thousands of looters are breaking windows and ripping away metal gates from storefronts in Harlem, the Bronx, Bushwick and Jamaica...'

'Jesus. It must be fuckin crazy in Jamaica. I bet the first thing they go for are the air conditioners.' He looks toward Jamaica, less than two miles east.

Denise sits up. 'Joe, I better get going. My father'll be wondering where I am since the lights went out.'

'What are ya gonna tell em?'

'I'll make something up.'

On the street it's more like a festival than a blackout. Whole families are out on their stoops with candles, flashlights and lanterns. Some are even having barbecues right out on the sidewalk. A bunch of shouting kids are marching down 106th Street led by a drum major with a Coleman lantern in one hand and a broken-off car antenna in the other.

Denise's parents are sitting on their stoop, which seems uncomfortably close to the playground they just left. When her father sees them coming, he drops a cigarette into an empty Piels can and walks out to the sidewalk to meet them, wielding a flashlight. He first shines it in Denise's face, then in Joe's, looking at them as if he knew what they've been doing for the past two hours. But he doesn't ask. Instead, he looks at Joe's green uniform shirt and asks him if maybe he knows when the lights will come back on. Joe says no, he doesn't, and the man goes back to the stoop and opens another beer.

Joe whispers to Denise that he'd better get going. She goes over to the stoop and gets him a candle. When she hands it to him she squeezes his hand.

'Good night, Hunter. Visit me again. Soon.'

On the way home Joe decides that it would probably be better if he didn't see Denise again. She'd probably want to get all involved and he couldn't handle that. Not with Rosie and all. And besides, there's a rule that Sal taught him. Sal D'Aurio, who owned the butcher shop Joe worked in when he was in high school, was married but never had less than half a dozen girlfriends at one time.

'But I never screw around in my own neighborhood,' he told Joe. 'You never shit where you eat.' Joe, now heading down 109th Street, figures, *Yeah, Sal was probably right.*

When Joe gets home he finds a box of candles and a note from Rosie on the table.

I went over to Frank and Linda's. Didn't want to be alone in the dark. Don't open the fridge or everything will go bad.

He blows out the candle and sits in the dark. He swallows to moisten his dry throat.

Something rises in his chest like a word that wants to come out. It rises, thick as a fist, up into his neck, then sinks back down.

In the lightless silence, so quiet–not even the refrigerator going on and off–there's only the chair he's sitting on to remind him that he is, in fact, somewhere. In fact, home.

Joe. Joe The Engineer. Husband. Meter reader. He keeps swallowing.

There's a portable TV to his left, though he can't see it, a chair with Rosie's tennis sneakers under it in the corner, where it was last night.

The door downstairs clicks open. A second later a flashlight beam hits the wall at the top of the stairs.

'Rosie?'

'You're home.'

'ROSIE?' he yells to her as she walks up the stairs.

'Yeah?'

'We can't even turn on the air conditioner... an it's so fuckin goddam hot.'

9

ON THE CORNER of Sutphin Boulevard and Jamaica Avenue, a pink stuffed dog is propped up between an el pillar and an overturned trash can. It is sitting up, three feet tall, its front paws, white underneath, extended forward.

Joe Flushing Avenue is staring in disbelief at a block of open, gutted storefronts. They're cruising down the avenue on their way out to Flushing and could have taken a half-dozen faster routes, but they wanted to see the looted storefronts in Jamaica.

'Cocksuckers sure did it up good,' he says to Joe, who is staring out the passenger window at the same scene across the street.

'I've seen enough,' Joe answers. 'Let's get off Jamaica. Take side streets ... anything.'

It's Friday morning. Joe and Rosie spent the day before in Frank and Linda's backyard. They barbecued all the frozen food they could eat and threw out the rest. Frank brought out the last of the corn from New Jersey, and Joe told him that the corn from the A & P tasted better. Just as night fell the lights came back on.

'Where were you when the lights went out?' Joe Flushing Avenue asks.

'Playin handball.'

'You're fulla shit.'

'I was... ' Joe looks at him sitting there, his stomach rising under the steering wheel, his wide fingers wrapped around it, smiling more to himself than to Joe, unshaven. Sometimes when Joe looks at him, a wave of fear passes through him. It's as if he is seeing a terminal illness he might get if he's not careful.

'You're fulla shit.'

'I was. I mean it. Where were you?'

'In Mary's. Her cousin Manny was there. Ya know, the fag from Brooklyn. He was lookin for somebody ta give a blowjob to.'

They stop at a light. Joe asks Joe Flushing Avenue to wait and jumps out to buy a newspaper. It's the first paper on the stands since Wednesday night when the lights went out, and the headline, two-inch letters over a photo of the crumbling front wall of a burnt-out furniture factory in Brooklyn, reads: A CITY RAVAGED.

'Anyway, Manny asks me if I play golf an I say no, so he says that's funny, ya look like the type. Can ya believe it? Me? Anyway just when he's tellin me *I look like the type*, the lights go. It was crazy for a moment but Mary had some candles in the back. Then Johnny ran home an got his Coleman lantern an it was business as usual. Ten beers later my own lights were out anyway... '

He looks over and sees Joe reading the paper.

'*You* bastard.'

'What?'

'I'll give ya somethin ya'll have ta listen to,' and he sticks his head out of the window, still driving, and lets out a fart that persists, without interruption, for the next two blocks.

part two

August 11–19

10

ALONG THE WALL opposite the bar in Mary's is a row of booths from the old days when Mary and her husband, Sonny, served food. That was before Sonny's drinking got so bad he couldn't cook anymore.

Joe still has the calendar they gave out back in 1960 when they first opened. He keeps it on the bathroom wall. It's yellowed and wrinkled from years of bathroom moisture and Rosie wants to throw it out, but he insists on keeping it. On the top there's a picture of a blonde in a low-cut pink gown holding a bouquet of pink roses. To her left, in gold letters, it says, *Pink Lady*. Underneath, just over the pages of months, it says, *Compliments of Mary's Bar and Grill—Home of the Famous Hero You Can Eat With a Knife and Fork.* Under that is the address and the phone number they used for takeout orders.

Now all you can get to eat at Mary's are beer nuts and Slim Jims, and no one uses the booths except couples, pool shooters sitting for a moment between shots and Johnny

Lemons, who converted the back booth into a sales counter for hot merchandise. He sells anything that can fall off a truck or be thrown over a fence. The back booth is referred to as Johnny's Discount Store, and at one time or another he's carried practically anything you can find in Macy's — portable TVs, Van Heusens, cassette recorders, boxed candy, ladies' stockings, wristwatches, Tiny Tears dolls — all at half price.

Tonight he's got a Sony portable, a Mickey Mouse telephone, a pair of women's deerskin gloves and a dozen gold pen and pencil sets he's had for six months and still can't unload.

Joe walks in, nods hello to Johnny and settles onto a stool. Joe Flushing Avenue is behind the bar, wearing an apron, wiping the counter top and singing like Jackie Gleason.

'Hello, Mr. Dunahee.'

'What the fuck are you doin?'

'Givin Mary some time off.'

'I was hopin ya quit your day job.'

'Joe Flushing Avenue pulls a beer for Joe and leans toward him.

'They took Sonny ta the hospital last night. That's where Mary is now. It's real bad. Cancer. The stomach.'

'Jesus.'

'She told him it was ulcers but she's sure he knows.'

'You seen em?'

'Yeah. Today. I couldn' believe it. A big man like Sonny. Jesus, he's down ta nothin.'

Sonny used to play cards with Joe's father. Every Thursday night for maybe ten years. Then his drinking got worse and he stopped showing up.

Joe never felt particularly close to Sonny, but he was a star in the constellation of adults that formed around him when he was growing up. When one goes out it always gets darker.

Sonny would be at Mary's at five in the morning to set up the kitchen and receive deliveries. During the last year before Mary closed up the kitchen, the same year he stopped showing up at the Thursday night card games, he'd crack open his first six-pack before the sun came up. By ten he'd have brought a fifth of something back to the kitchen from the bar, and by midafternoon, no matter what you ordered, he'd put up french fries.

During the last five or six years nobody'd even seen Sonny. Mary refers to the years before that as the time before 'my husband got sick.' Sometimes she'd talk to Joe Flushing Avenue about it. Sometimes she'd leave the bar for a half hour or so and try to feed him something, or peel him off the kitchen table, or the floor, or the toilet, and put him to bed.

Before they opened Mary's Bar and Grill, Sonny was the head cook at Longchamps Restaurant. He was the only cook, he used to tell Joe, that Mayor Wagner would allow to make his lunch when he came there.

Joe walks over to Johnny's booth and checks out his merchandise. Johnny tells him he just got a gas barbecue. Beautiful.

'Ya wanna take a look? I got it in the car.'

'Nah.'

Joe picks up the deerskin gloves and slips them out of the box. They're a soft tan and lined with rabbit fur. They'd probably fit Rosie.

'How much?'

'I'll take ten.'

'You'll take five.'

'They're imported. From Switzerlan. I tell ya what. Seven-fifty.'

'If they was American I might pay more.' Joe drops them on the table.

'Six.'

'No thanks.' He turns back toward the bar.

'Awright already. Five.'

'Sold.'

He brings the gloves back to his seat at the bar. Joe Flushing Avenue pulls a fresh beer for both of them and picks up the box with the gloves.

'Nice stuff.'

'Yeah.'

'How much ya pay?'

'Five.'

'I could got em for three.'

'You couldna got em for ten.'

Joe Flushing Avenue calls to Johnny that Joe wants to buy him a beer on account of him making such a good deal and all. He takes the money from the bills sitting in front of Joe on the bar, puts it in the register, then comes back and smiles at him.

'They for Rosie?'

'Uh huh.'

'That's a nice husband.'

'Shove it.'

'Why don't ya get something for Florence?'

'Why don't *you* get somethin for Florence? Johnny's got a phone over there that looks like Mickey Mouse. She'd love it. When ya call her up and ask her for a date she can tell ya no right through Mickey's hand.'

Mary walks in. Her dress is rumpled like she slept in it. She hasn't changed her makeup in two days and looks older and more tired than Joe has ever seen her look.

'Mary, how's Sonny?' Joe asks her.

'He's sleepin now. They're gonna give him treatments but they're not hopeful. They haven't said nothin but I can tell.'

'Mary, why don't ya go home,' Joe Flushing Avenue

tells her. 'I'll stay around tonight and close up.'

She thanks him but tells him she'll stay. She pours herself a cup of coffee and sits in one of the booths, where she pulls out her compact and puts on fresh makeup. She sits for a minute sipping her coffee, then takes out her compact again and checks her makeup in the mirror. Joe Flushing Avenue asks her if she's sure she doesn't want him to close up for her. She says no thanks, gets up and goes behind the bar. After pulling another beer for him and Joe, she sits back and stares at the TV.

'Ya want me ta change the channel?' Joe Flushing Avenue asks her.

'Nah.'

'How about the sound? Ya want me ta turn up the sound?'

'No thanks. It's okay.'

After his beer Joe heads for the door. On his way out Johnny asks him what day his wedding anniversary falls on.

'November seventh.'

'What year?'

'Seventy-two.'

'Lemme see. That's eleven... seven... seventy-two.'

'That's right.'

He knows Johnny has no intention of giving him and Rosie an anniversary present. He just needs a new set of numbers to bet on. Johnny feels that birthdays, wedding anniversaries, license plate numbers, the ages of a friend's children, any number with a real person somewhere behind it, any number that quantifies something, has to be luckier than any colorless, odorless, inorganic group of digits he simply pulls out of the air.

11

JOE LIKES THE IDEA of bringing Rosie a pair of gloves. It will please her. And he knows that he often doesn't please Rosie. But bringing the gloves, a relatively simple thing to do, will please her.

He's still deeply attracted to Rosie but he doesn't always realize it. He doesn't have the opportunity to watch her walking down the street, twenty feet ahead of him, like a woman he doesn't know, and try to imagine her life. Somehow, for both of them, the narrowing of distance has stopped being an urgent matter. It's hard, after five years to always remember. Rosie's still attracted to him too. He can feel it. That's one way they still please each other.

Only now, the sex he likes best is the sex that's the least involved, that changes him the least from the state he's in before it happens. He likes to be lying on the couch watching TV, and then if Rosie comes into the room, say to her, 'Ya have ta give me a blowjob right away or my cock'll fall off,' and sometimes she does it. Just saying it turns him on. He also likes to sneak up behind her when she's washing the dishes and slip his hand under her blouse. Sometimes she'll pull away and sometimes she'll turn her head and smile and he'll go on. He'll tug down her jeans or pull her panties out from under her white waitresss dress and slip it in from behind. He likes to do it fast. He likes to enter her before her hands are even out of the dishwasher.

The gloves are a good idea. They'll please her.

Most of the sidewalk on 109th Street was laid in the late forties when young couples, escaping the glacial advance of the poor in Brooklyn and Manhattan, bought up the old turn-of-the-century houses with GI mortgages. They built garages, replaced coal furnaces with oil burners, seeded front lawns, and closed in the old wooden front porches that had rotted from years of exposure until ferns burst through their dried crossboards.

A crack between the paving squares starts at Atlantic Avenue and runs, without interruption, for an easy fifty feet, where it meets a larger concrete slab, laid earlier or later, breaking the tile-like sequence, and ends, like a side street that runs into an avenue but doesn't continue beyond the other side. Almost every night Joe follows this crack on his way home, head down, like a bomber strafing the Ho Chi Minh Trail, till he comes to the crossline. When he gets there he takes another three steps forward, then four to the right, and he's at the front stoop of the house he and Rosie rent the top floor of.

Rosie's lying on the couch, reading. Her feet, in peds, are crossed on the arm.

The house is silent. It seems to Joe that whenever he's not in the apartment for a while it slows down. Then it speeds up and fills with noises as soon as he gets home.

'What are ya readin?' The gloves are in his back pocket.

'Henry Miller. Iris lent it ta me.'

'I heard a him. Didn't he marry Marilyn Monroe?'

'No. That was Arthur Miller.'

'Oh yeah, Arthur Miller.'

He goes into the bathroom, takes off his shirt and washes up. When he comes back to the living room, he tells Rosie that they took Sonny to the hospital.

'What's wrong with him?'

'Cancer.'

'That's too bad. What's Mary gonna do?'

'I don't know.'

'After all those years of drinking I'm not surprised it didn't happen sooner.'

Joe feels something personal in how Rosie brings up Sonny's drinking.

'Who knows how he got it.'

'That's probably why.'

Joe goes into the kitchen, lays the gloves on the kitchen table and turns on the portable TV.

'Is the air conditioner workin?' he yells back into the living room. 'It doesn't feel like it's workin so good.'

'I think it needs a new filter.'

'Yeah.'

Rosie gets up and comes into the kitchen. She leans up against Joe and stares at the TV screen.

'Have you thought about the vacation?'

'Nah.'

'What's this?' Rosie picks up the gloves. 'For me?'

'Uh huh.'

She takes them out of the box, puts them on, takes them off, rubs the lining against her cheek.

'They're beautiful. I wish it was cold so I could wear em.'

'I wish it was cold too.'

Next Monday begins their two-week vacation. Rosie wants to go away for at least a week. Iris and Roger rented

a small place just outside of Woodstock for the whole
summer and invited them up for as long as they wanted to
stay. Joe wants to stay home and go fishing.

He goes back into the living room and lies on the couch,
still warm from Rosie lying on it.

He doesn't particularly love fishing but it reminds him of
his father's vacations. He used to take Joe and his brother,
James, to Broad Channel. They'd rent a rowboat, row a
few hundred yards out into the channel and catch porgies,
hackleheads, bragalls, eels and an occasional snapper.
Once when they were anchored maybe twenty yards from
the Cross Bay Bridge, an E train passed over it, the
windows crammed with workers on their way from the
Rockaways to Manhattan, and Joe's father stood up,
opened his fly and started pissing for all the commuters to
see. 'You poor slobs,' he yelled, 'havin ta go ta work. Look
at me. I'm on vacation!' Since then Joe always associates
fishing with vacations.

Rosie comes in and rubs the glove over Joe's cheek, then
his chest.

'Well, have you thought about it?'

'About what?'

'Goin up ta Iris and Roger's.'

'Why don't we stay home and go fishing. We'll go ta
Broad Channel. Every day. When the train comes we'll
piss off the boat.'

Rosie knows the story. She hears it every year.

'We stayed home last year.' She rubs the glove, lining
turned out, over his chest and stomach.

'Yeah. It was real restful, wasn't it?'

'Nope.' She notices a bulge on the inside of his thigh and
slides the glove over it. 'We'll just go for a week.'

Joe doesn't answer. She opens his fly, lifts out his cock
and places the glove over it.

'Fits like a glove,' he says.

'Just for a week.'

'It' s a rubber we can use five times. Let's try it out.' He pulls her on top of him and lifts her skirt over her hips. He sees the middle finger of the glove poking up behind her from between her legs. 'I'll make a deal,' he says. 'One weekend.'

He pulls the glove off and watches the tip of his cock poking out over her ass. Rosie begins to move.

'It looks like the sun setting and rising.'

'What?' she asks, laughing.

'It looks like the sun, I said.'

'Five days,' Rosie answers.

'Okay, five days.'

On her way to the bedroom Rosie opens the bathroom door and yells to Joe, who's in the shower, to remember to shut off the living room light and the air conditioner before he goes to bed. A second later she's back at the door and shouts to forget the living room light, she'll get it if he'll just remember the air conditioner.

Even though they just made love, he jerks off in the shower. He does that sometimes. Something builds up in him that takes more than one orgasm to get out and sometimes he likes the second one privately.

He also thinks about what he's getting himself into with this vacation. In a way it's a good idea, so he can see what Iris and Rosie are up to. They've been spending a lot of time together lately, a lot more than they used to, and there's something about it, something he can't quite put his finger on, that bothers him. Sometimes she takes the subway into the city at night and sometimes she stays after work. Once she stayed over, calling Joe to tell him it was easier than coming home late and a lot closer to work in the morning. He doesn't like her coming home looking like she had a good time that he had nothing to do with. He tells her he doesn't like her riding the subway alone at night, and she invites him to come along. This confuses him more. Her behaving like there's nothing unusual going on, nothing at all unlike the things they do when they're together. He gets paranoid too, thinking maybe she knows he won't come.

Dealing with Roger will be the hard part. Last week he called Rosie at Iris's and Roger answered the phone. As soon as he heard Roger's voice, he was reaching for his pants, the first step in a chain of events that would start him running over to Mary's to borrow Johnny's knuckles and Joe Flushing Avenue's car, and end with him standing in front of Iris's apartment waiting for Roger to open the door. But then Roger told him that Rosie was on her way home. They'd been to a lecture at the New School and she left a halfhour ago. Joe asked him why they went to a lecture and Roger told him they had a sudden urge to learn something.

'Don't you ever get the urge?' he asked Joe.

'Yeah,' he told him. 'That's why I got a fuckin encyclopedia,' and hung up.

When Rosie got home he asked her if Roger was always there when she visited.

'Not usually. He lives upstairs. Sometimes he comes down after I leave.'

'What about the night ya stayed over?'

'They both went upstairs and I had the whole place to myself.'

Avoid them both. That'll be the best thing to do. He'll bring a fishing pole. Two. He'll buy one for Rosie. They'll spend the entire five days fishing. That's it. They probably won't come along. He'd like to see Iris squeeze a worm onto a hook.

He imagines their arrival. Iris and Roger picking them up at the bus station. Joe in a hat with fishing lures stuck into it, with a tackle box and a fish pouch on his belt. Rosie in hip boots, carrying a fly rod.

'Oh, ya don't fish? We were hopin ya might come along. Oh well. Too bad. Ya won't mind droppin us off at the nearest stream, would ya? Trout don't wait all day. And by the way, we might be back late so don't wait up.'

He dries himself off and lies down on the bed. Then he remembers the air conditioner, gets up, turns it off, opens the window, gets back into bed on top of the sheets and tries to fall asleep before the heat takes over the room.

12

JOE AND JOE FLUSHING AVENUE are passing through Richmond Hill on their way out to South Ozone Park. They've been reading South O Z for a week now and have another week to go. An ad for Lip Quencher comes over the radio. It uses the same theme song as the TV commercial, and they both immediately flash to the blonde, who lately has been showing up at least three times during Johnny Carson, licking her glistening red lips, which, in the closing shot, fill the entire screen.

'What makes wet lips so sexy, I wonder,' Joe Flushing Avenue thinks out loud in the tone of voice he thinks out loud in when he knows he's going to answer his own question. 'Maybe it makes em look like they just gave somebody a blowjob. Whaddayou think?' he asks Joe.

'About what?' Joe answers.

'What I was sayin. About the wet look.'

'Yeah, you're probably right.'

'Yeah. It's the blowjob look. Gets me every time.'

It's August 12th and there isn't a cloud in the sky. According to the radio, it's 9:45 and already eighty-nine WABC degrees.

They stop at the light on the corner of 111th Street and Atlantic. There's a line of women forming out in front of Furci's Bingo Hall waiting for the doors to open at ten o'clock.

Your own neighborhood is a weird place to find yourself on a weekday midmorning. It feels like you're not supposed to be there. Even though the surroundings are familiar — Ed's Candy Store, the worn yellow and blue gas pumps on the J & R Sunoco lot — Joe's encased in a car and a job, and responds to Richmond Hill with the same indifference, the same disdain he's felt toward all the other neighborhoods he's passed through on nearly every weekday morning for the past five years.

He watches the slow stream of blocks. The old Norway maples and sycamores, the fronts of the houses, the bus stops every two blocks or so with three or four women waiting on each one, the older ones with shopping bags, the younger ones with children or both. If it weren't for the parked cars, which date the streets, you might think the Second World War has just ended.

When Joe went to school he envied the women who lived on his block for having the daylight hours all to themselves. While he had to spend his day stuck in a classroom that smelled like chalk dust and rotten apples, they were free to spend their mornings watching TV, hanging clothes, sipping coffee on Formica kitchen counters, or just standing out front in shifts or bathrobes and house slippers, talking.

The sky this morning is a clear, deep blue, which is the color it always is when you're not free to walk around under it.

One of Joe's earliest memories is of sitting in a plastic

washtub in the backyard while his mother was hanging clothes. He's not sure anymore if he remembers it directly or if he remembers remembering it at some chronological midpoint of twelve or thirteen. There was a portable radio that had a wire running through the bedroom window and was bigger than the nonportable radios of today. The center of the memory, the impression that has stayed intact with the most clarity, is the blue of the sky. His mother reeled the clothes out over the grass and then stopped. At that moment his mind took a picture of clean white nightgown and diaper-shaped spaces cut out of an incredibly dazzling blue.

It's the same blue he remembers seeing out the windows of classrooms and army barracks. The same blue he will remember if he remembers this morning, shining over Furci's Bingo Hall, and all the women waiting on busy stops, and the car with the words *Brooklyn/Queens Water Resources* stenciled on both doors, and the ten square blocks of one- to three-family houses whose basements he will spend the day walking around in.

They cross Rockaway Boulevard and Joe Flushing Avenue starts doing the Gas Pedal Blues along with Frank Sinatra singing 'My Way.' He presses the pedal to the floor with one beat, then lifts his foot off completely with the next. The other cars on the street slow down or speed up to increase their distance. Joe tells him to cut it out, he's getting seasick.

'But I'm doin it *my* way.'

'Fine. If I throw up I'll aim it *your* way.'

Joe Flushing Avenue evens off on the gas and the car stops leapfrogging. Gradually the other cars, sensing that the danger is over, speed up again. As they pass they look at Joe and Joe Flushing Avenue as if they're crazy. One guy pulls up next to them at a light, leans out of the passenger window and asks Joe Flushing Avenue if he thinks he's the only car on the road. Joe Flushing Avenue tells him he looks familiar.

'Oh yeah?' the guy says, forgetting he's supposed to be mad.

'Yeah. Now I think I remember. You an your wife got a wedding picture on your dresser, right?'

He scratches his head. 'I think so.'

'Yeah. That's where I saw ya. Your wife showed it ta me... right after I fucked her. An ya know what? Ya haven't changed a bit.'

Joe starts laughing. The guy tells Joe he doesn't think his fat friend is so funny. Joe Flushing Avenue pulls his flashlight off his belt, leans out the window and takes a swing at his head. The guy decides to roll up his window, even though it's eighty-nine WABC degrees, and makes a left at the next corner.

Once they cross Linden Boulevard they're in their sector. In South O Z there's nothing higher than three stories, so you can see all of it from anywhere in it or near it. From the second floor you can see Jamaica Bay, which you can smell even when you're down in the basements.

Neighborhoods like this one have their good and bad points. The good being that they are relatively safe and you know what to expect when you ring a doorbell. The bad being that there isn't one apartment house in the whole sector. In ten square blocks of apartment houses you read maybe sixty meters. With private homes it's more like three hundred.

They park the car at the end of the fourth block of the sector, which is where they expect to end up at lunchtime. Then they head back to the first street, each with a deck of meter cards. Joe has the even addresses and Joe Flushing Avenue the odd ones. The temperature has climbed at least five degrees and the sky has grown as radiant as Technicolor over the dull-shingled housetops. Without a word they split and head up different sides of the street.

13

THE THIRD HOUSE on 135th Street off Linden Boulevard has a big V written in a curly band of aluminum across its screen door.

Mrs. Voletsky, who is wearing a green quilted house-coat, is in her early fifties and suspicious. The air that escapes when she opens the door is a thick mixture of coffee, air conditioning and vinyl upholstery.

'Yeah?' she says to Joe, who is not the mailman or the paper boy and therefore potentially dangerous.

Joe smiles. He knows her well. She came out of the last house he went to and she'll come out of the one next door.

'Water Resources, ma'am. Come ta read your meter.'

'Water man? You haven't been here for a year.'

'That's right, ma'am. One year, ta be exact.'

'How come we gotta pay for water anyway?'

She's not letting him down. It's the same conversation he'll have at every doorstep in the neighborhood.

'Ya get a piece of the reservoir, ya gotta pay for it.'

Then he walks up to her and shows her the meter card. He shines his flashlight on it, a completely unnecessary thing to do in the bright morning, but it forms a little theatrical spot around the name, VOLETSKY, with a little dash under each letter, RALPH.

She's somewhat impressed, seeing her husband's name spotlighted on the card held for her by this stranger. Mr. Voletsky's at his job, Joe figures, and judging by the two-family house he has all to himself, he probably does a lot worse to people than read their water meters.

'An there's a space for more information on this card than water consumption. Like if there are any violations an if the resident is cooperative.'

She goes back to being unimpressed and motions to the alley around the left side of the house.

'It's open,' she says and slips back inside.

Sometimes weird things happen when you go down into people's basements. Last year a Japanese family out in Flushing wouldn't even let him go down the cellar steps until he took his shoes off.

He once walked right into the middle of a cockfight without knowing it until he got right up to the edge of the pit and saw the two roosters, with shining metal spurs, tearing each other apart. It was under an apartment house in Jamaica. There were ten or twelve guys standing around the pit who were so absorbed in the fight that they didn't notice Joe till he was standing next to them and then they thought he was some kind of cop with his flashlight and green uniform. It took him some time to convince them that he wasn't, and once he did he decided to approximate the building's water consumption and beat it the hell out of there.

Some guy in Woodhaven had one entire wall of his basement lined with portable TVs stacked four or five

high. It looked like a department store showroom. There
were at least a hundred of them but Joe didn't ask any
questions. He's supposed to report things like cockfights
and excessive collections of household appliances but he
never does. He has his business, they have theirs.

The Voletskys' basement is nothing special. It's as long
as the house, with a workbench in the back and a sink and
washing machine in the front. The whole left-hand side,
running lengthwise, is enclosed and finished. The unfinished half has poured concrete floors and the foundation of
the house for walls.

He finds the meter on the wall over the sink next to the
electric and gas meters. The sink smells like someone
recently cleaned fish in it. There's a black rubber hose
running into it from the washing machine, which is
throbbing regularly. The meter registers thirty-five units
consumed since last August. That's thirty-five units at
seven hundred square feet of water per unit, which tells Joe
that Mrs. Voletsky and family probably spend half their
day in the shower and the other half watering the lawn. As
he's writing down the numbers, the washing machine hits a
rinse cycle, begins to spin and rock and then suddenly a
wad of suds gushes out of the black hose into the sink. Joe
jumps back, then looks up at the ceiling, which is in Mrs.
Voletsky's general direction, as if she had something to do
with the timing.

Going down into the basements of perfect strangers is
nothing to look forward to. But once you're down there
and you're by yourself and you can just walk around for a
while looking at things, it can stop being a job. Just for a
short while. It's like looking through a family album, only
better.

The door leading to the finished area is open and he
walks in. The floor is tiled and the walls are covered with

cherry-red plywood paneling. Mr Voletsky must like Clydesdale horses because there are a half-dozen prints of them along the walls pulling beer wagons. On one end of the room is a small bar, also cherry red, and three aluminum and red vinyl stools. Over the bar is a clock with a drunken clown face. The hands stem from his red, swollen nose. Across his hatband it says, *Bar Closes at 4 A.M.*, and there's no number in the spot where the four usually is. The dozen varied bottles all have little-boy pourers, the kind that piss out the liquor when you tilt the bottle.

Across the room is a couch that was probably their living room couch before they got their new one and a TV which was probably their last living room TV. On the couch, next to a wide, crater-like impression, is an accordion. Joe imagines them having a poor fat twelve-year-old son who they force to take accordion lessons and then make him practice down here, where nobody can hear him. He sees him sitting there, filling the impression on the couch, grunting over 'Lady of Spain' and trying to turn the pages of music at the same time. Meanwhile Mrs. Voletsky would be upstairs taking her third shower of the day while Ralph, home from work, waters the lawn.

Joe walks back out into the cooler, unfinished area. All sorts of things are hanging from nails along the rafters. A pair of ski boots, probably belonging to an older son, who might even be old enough to have gotten laid already and is definitely old enough, unlike the poor chubby accordionist imprisoned in the other room, to politely tell his parents to shove it if they try to force music lessons on him. There's also a bicycle tire, a yardstick and a dozen dusty, brown-paper-wrapped parcels shaped like teapots, electric train cars and birdcages.

Coming down to within two feet of the sink is a flight of stairs that probably leads up to the kitchen. Under the steps is a stand-up freezer and an old clothes closet with its doors removed and shelves built into it that are lined with canned food, paper towels, stacks of aluminium pie trays and Mason jars.

Farther along the same wall is an old dark wood dresser. Joe opens the two small top drawers, which probably once held the delicate things that went next to her skin when there was less of it and it was softer. Now one of them holds old nutcrackers, an eggbeater, which has probably since been replaced by a Mixmaster, a broken screwdriver, and an old set of silverware, the knives, forks and spoons each wrapped in several rubber bands. The other top drawer is crammed with folded, mothball-smelling linens.

Sometimes when he's walking around like this in somebody's basement, he walks out of himself for a while and just wanders around in their lives. He stops being a person who, like Mrs. Voletsky or anyone else, is completely absorbed in the things they do and own. He likes the feeling. He becomes a ghost.

He wishes he could make it happen but he never knows when it's going to. It's something you can't plan. You just slide out of your life. Haunting someone else's basement is a lot easier than being in your own life. It's a rest. A vacation.

When he hears the door upstairs crack open, sending a shaft of light down the steps and against the sink, he laughs.

'Are you still there? . . . Hey . . . water man . . . Are you still there?'

He slips back into himself, like Certs the breath mint and Certs the candy mint, and laughs quietly.

'Are you still there?'

He could make something up. Like he's checking the pipes or replacing a part in the meter but he sneaks out into the alley and leaves her to wonder.

Out front, just fifteen or twenty feet up the street, the width of a driveway, is another front door and another bell to ring.

CAPUANO, MICHAEL. The Capuanos don't have a C on their screen door. But they do have a black wooden cat sitting in a bed of ivy on their lawn with a white C painted in the curve of its body.

Mrs. Capuano also wants to know how come she has to pay for water and Joe tells her she doesn't. She can drill her own well and install a pump if she wants to, or drive out to a lake once a week and store the water in her bathtub, or put a barrel under her rain gutter, or water her rosebushes with Coca-Cola. But if she didn't want to do any of these things, she would have to let Joe go downstairs and read her meter. He shows her the card. He shines his flashlight on the name–see? CAPUANO–and then he shows her all the other spaces on the card where he writes down any violations and whether the above-named resident has been cooperative or not.

14

JOE WALKS IN and finds Iris standing next to the couch in one of Rosie's two-piece bathing suits. It's too small for her and the top heaves up her breasts like a Marie Antoinette pushup bra while the bottom squeezes a small roll of flesh up over the waistband. He looks at her. She looks back at him like he just wandered into a dressing room at Bloomingdale's.

Rosie walks in from the bedroom carrying another bathing suit, a blue one-piece. She says hello to Joe and hands it to Iris.

'Try this one,' she says.

Iris breaks her stare from Joe, takes the new bathing suit and goes into the bedroom.

'Iris doesn't have one,' Rosie tells Joe, 'so I'm lending her one of mine. She's been swimming in short shorts and a T-shirt all summer, so I told her how could anybody get a suntan much less swim in shorts.' She shakes her head. 'What's that?' she adds, pointing to a flat, rectangular box

Joe has pressed under his arm.

'Air conditioner filter.'

'Oh good. You remembered.'

'If all your bathin suits fit her like that one maybe she oughtta wear shorts.'

'Don't be nasty.'

'Don't be *honest*, ya mean.'

'Be good. She's gonna have dinner with us... an stay over too.'

'Great.'

Iris comes out of the bedroom in the blue one-piece. It has the same Marie Antoinette effect on the top but this time squeezes her out at the bottom.

Joe passes her on his way into the bedroom with the new filter. They still haven't exchanged a word.

They have dinner at Jahn's on 118th Street. Joe and Rosie used to go there a lot before he got drafted. If you go on your birthday, and can produce a birth certificate, they give you a free sundae. There are four Jahn's restaurant-ice-cream parlors in Queens. On Joe's nineteenth birthday he and Rosie went to all of them. They haven't gone there much during the last few years.

The one in Richmond Hill is the original Jahn's, built in 1897, and it still has its Gay Nineties look. Red patterned wallpaper made to look and feel like real velvet, deep Leatherette chairs in the booths, wooden tables with initials carved in them that date back to the twenties, and old streetlamps, street signs and stop-and-go traffic signals at the ends of the aisles. In the back room there's an old nickelodeon with musical instruments in it that really play when you put a dime in.

They sit in the back room at the same table Joe carved his and Rosie's initials in on their way home from a New Year's Eve party seven years ago. She points it out to Iris.

J L. & R.V. 1/1/70. Iris says it's cute. Joe says, yeah, real cute.

Underneath on their initials it says, *JACKIE B. U.S.N. WAS HERE ON LEAVE U.S.S. NEW JERSEY 11/2/43.* Underneath Jackie B.'s message is a coiled rattlesnake with its forked tongue sticking out.

Joe has an open meat-loaf sandwich, Rosie the veal cutlets and Iris a chef's salad. Afterwards Rosie and Iris have coffee and Joe has a hot fudge sundae that Rosie picks at with her teaspoon.

'Have some,' Joe says to Iris.

'No thanks, I'm watching my weight.'

Rosie gives Joe a warning look just in case he plans on agreeing with her.

When the check comes Iris offers to pay but Joe won't let her. He picks it up and won't even let her see it.

'One thing I ain't is cheap,' he says.

'I know that,' Iris says, not knowing if by offering to pay she had somehow accused him of it.

'Let me tell ya a story about somebody I knew who was really cheap,' he says.

'Do ya have to?' Rosie asks.

'Ya wanna hear it, don't ya, Iris?'

'I guess.'

'Good,' Joe says.

'Yeah, terrific,' Rosie says.

'Yeah, good,' Joe says again. 'Anyway, the guy's name was Tony Pug.'

'Tony Pugliese,' Rosie clarifies for Iris.

'Yeah. Anyway, this guy Tony was tighter than a frog's ass an a frog's ass is watertight. He was always bummin dimes and quarters for somethin. When we were collectin for beer he always showed us how empty the insides of his pockets were. Whenever we drove out ta Rockaway he would miraculously fall asleep a half-mile from the tollbooth an then wake up just after we passed it. If ya ever asked him to pay back the money he owed ya he'd say, sure, just as soon as my father goes back ta work. Meanwhile his father was a fireman who fell through the roof of a burnin house an broke his back when Tony was fifteen an everybody knew he wasn't ever goin back ta work. If ya said ta Tony, why don't ya get a job? he'd say, I'm waiting for the right opportunity. He was always waitin for the right opportunity...'

The waitress comes by and asks if anybody wants more coffee. Joe asks if they all want to go over to Mary's for a drink afterwards, but they say no. He asks for a glass of water.

'So anyway, one day we were playin basketball over in the Hundred and Sixth Street park an afterwards we stop at Al's Sunoco on Atlantic Avenue ta get some soda from the machine. Nobody's got any money for Tony so he takes big sips outta everybody else's.

'When we leave, this guy Ralphie Fitzgerald hangs behind, only nobody knows what he's doin...'

Joe leans closer so Iris can hear.

'See, he walks over ta the curb an when Al's fillin up a car and can't see him he scrapes up a piece of dog shit with a matchbook and puts it in the coin return slot. Then when we were maybe halfway up the block he stops and says, oh shit, I forgot my change... Ya see in those days a can a soda only cost twenny cents, so if ya put in a quarter ya got a nickel back... Anyway, Tony takes off like somebody shot him out of a gun and heads back ta the machine. He sticks his fingers inta the coin return slot expectin a nickel an pulls out a lump a wet dog shit.'

Rosie's laughing, even though she's heard it before. Iris smiles. Then looks like she's going to throw up. Then, seeing Rosie laugh, she smiles again.

Joe, thinking maybe the story has somehow cheered

them up, asks if they're sure they don't want to toss a couple down at Mary's but they still don't want to.

'Anyway, I'll finish the story.'

'There's more?' Iris asks.

'Sure,' Joe says. 'When I tell a story I don't short-change nobody.'

'Amen,' Rosie says.

'Anyway, I'll finish the story. Al sees Tony over by the Coke machine and sees the coin return all smeared with dog shit an comes over with a tire iron in his hand. Tony tried ta explain but Al wasn't hearin nothin. He just stood there holding the tire iron till Tony cleaned it out.

'The next day Tony fills a paper bag with dog shit, puts it on Ralphie's stoop, lights it up an rings the bell an runs. Only Ralphie don't come out. It was his father that answered the door and when he puts out the fire he gets dog shit all over his bedroom slippers.'

Iris wants to know if it's a true story. Joe tells her of course it's true.

'And what happened to this Tony?'

'For about two weeks he stopped hangin out. Then he started comin around like usual. In no time he was grubbing money again. About a year later he went inta the reserves. After that he joined the post office. I haven't heard from him since.'

On the way home they stop in front of Mary's. Joe asks if they're still sure they don't just want a quick one.

They look in the open door. Joe Flushing Avenue is behind the bar. He smiles, shouts hello to Rosie and waves for them to come in.

Iris looks around and Joe watches her look around. Joe Flushing Avenue leans over the bar. Johnny Lemons holds up a small portable TV in the back booth.

'It's got a radio too,' he yells. 'AM-FM!'

There are three men at the bar and two more playing pool. Joe watches Iris's eyes move along the swordfish on the wall over the bar and the big Slim Jim sign that eight years ago Sonny, as a joke, hung over the men's room door. The two guys at the pool table stare back at her. She looks afraid. Also like she's looking down a sewer that just backed up.

'I don't want to go in,' she says.

She looks at Joe, then at Rosie.

'We weren't gonna stop anyway,' Rosie says.

'What's the matter, Iris?' Joe asks her.

'It's late. I just want to go.'

Rosie sees what's coming and tries to take Iris by the arm and lead her away from the door. Joe Flushing Avenue is watching from the bar.

'What's the matter, Iris?' Joe asks again. 'Ain't this place good enough?'

Rosie leads Iris farther out onto the street.

'. . . An you too, Rosie?'

They turn and start walking away.

'Ta hell with yas both. I'm stayin.'

He goes over to the bar, sits down, then gets up and runs back out onto Atlantic Avenue.

'WHERE DO YOU HANG OUT?' he shouts at them, at Iris in particular, 'GAY BARS?'

Rosie turns around and gives Joe an 'up your's' sign. Then she turns, slips her arm through Iris's and they continue walking up the avenue.

He goes back inside and Joe Flushing Avenue sets a beer in front of him.

'Who's the little chickie with Rosie?'

Joe waves him away but he doesn't stay away.

'What's up?'

'I don't know. That bitch comes over. When I walk in she's tryin on all a Rosie's bathin suits. We eat supper. We walk over here The whole time she's lookin at me like I never took a bath in my life.'

'High society, hah? Fuck her.'

'Only she's got Rosie behavin real weird. Right now they're struttin down Atlantic Avenue arm in arm like a coupla lesbians or somethin.'

'Ya gotta have a talk with Rosie.'

'I'm gonna tell her who to hang out with?'

'Why not?'

'Cause I can't.'

'If ya haveta, give her a shot in the head. Ya can't have her carryin on like this. It ain't right. Give her a shot an she'll stop seein her mother if ya want her to.'

Joe goes over to a booth. Johnny Lemons comes over with his portable TV but Joe waves him away. For the next two hours he doesn't talk to anyone. He just leaves the booth for refills and bathroom runs.

When he gets home he expects Iris to be sleeping on the couch but the living room is empty. He thinks maybe they're both sleeping in the bedroom just to piss him off but they're not there either. There's no note on the kitchen table and no sign of them anywhere. He goes through all the rooms again.

'That bitch,' he says again. 'Fuck that bitch!'

He decides to sleep on the couch since he's standing right next to it. Before falling asleep he wonders what Rosie finds to like about Iris. When she's with that bitch she behaves like someone else... more and more... someone he can't talk to... someone he hardly knows.

That night he dreams that he and Rosie are on a bus, perhaps on their way up to Iris and Roger's summer place. Cows are grazing along the highway and Joe points them out to Rosie. They they drive past miles of cornfields, and Rosie says that if the bus would only stop they could get out and pick some for Frank and Linda. Joe tells her that Joe Flushing Avenue says men should beat their wives if they won't be the kind of wives they want them to be. He wants Rosie to know that he's not this kind of man. He's a different kind of man. It's important that she knows this. As he's telling her this, the bus drives off the road and flips over. It keeps rolling, sideways, down the shoulder of the road and out into a cornfield. When it stops, everyone else is dead but there are no bodies or blood or anything. Just Joe, standing next to the overturned bus, looking into the windows and not seeing anybody.

He wakes and looks up at the living room ceiling. Then he jumps off the couch and begins walking around and shaking his arms until he shakes off the dream.

When he is fully awake he takes a shower and then crawls into bed. He stretches his legs and arms so that his body covers Rosie's side of the bed too.

15

JOE'S SITTING on a bench in City Hall Park waiting for Rosie to get to work. It's 10:45 and he's been sitting there for about fifteen minutes. She works at Cassandra's, about half a block west on Barclay Street, and gets in at 11:00.

He's been watching a work crew, high up on scaffolding, sandblast the stone facade of the Woolworth Building. They've finished the upper third, which is now a sandy-clean tan. The remaining two thirds, running right down to street level, is a sooty brown with occasional darker seepage stains.

The first thing he did when he awoke, even before remembering the night before, was to pick up the phone, dial the office and tell Nettie, the receptionist, in his best early-morning-gravelly voice that he was sick. Something in him knew immediately upon waking that he wouldn't be going to work.

He's trying to figure out what Rosie's thinking. He wonders if last night he screwed up their chances of going up to Iris and Roger's summer place next week. That's okay with him, but it's important to Rosie. Maybe that's why she got so mad she just left and didn't even leave a note or call or anything.

Across from Joe a man is sleeping under an open *New York Post*. The headline reads: SON OF SAM CLAIMS HE HEARD VOICES. There are about a dozen bums, teenagers and various other people who are not among the stream of office workers, sitting around the fountain cooling off. Every five minutes at least a hundred people rush past in both directions. All of them going someplace, aimed and officious, absolutely sure of where it is they're going and what they'll do when they get there. Joe's more interested in the men up on the scaffolds, aiming their sandblasters like M-16s. He wonders if they make more than he does. It looks like much better work than reading water meters, being on the tops of buildings instead of underneath them.

He gets up and walks along the path that exits on Barclay Street. Could she be insulted for Iris? Could they be that much alike?

He passes two teenage boys on the path. One has a huge portable radio he needs a shoulder strap to carry and jeans that are so long the cuffs come back up again almost to his knees. They keep throwing a pair of sneakers up into the air, higher and higher, each time catching them by the laces, until finally they get tangled in the upper branches of an Ailanthus tree. They'd probably be a lot better off Joe figures, if they had a job.

When he gets to Cassandra's, Rosie's sitting at the last table of her section, filling sugar pourers from an aluminium pitcher with a funnel-like tube for a spout. He watches for a while before approaching. When she's working she never sits on a chair for support or comfort but rather for balance, with most of the weight still on her feet, ready to jump up at a moment's notice. She works fast and

methodically, like an assembly line. While she is pouring
the sugar with her left hand, she screws on the lid of the last
one filled and then unscrews the next one with her right.
When noon comes she has to be ready. After that she won't
have a spare second to refill anything.

Joe sits in the seat opposite hers. She's surprised to see
him but she smiles. He smiles too. She stops filling the
pourers but he tells her, no, go on and finish them. He has
no idea what she's thinking and no idea what to say. He
takes one of the filled pourers, unscrews the lid, licks his
fingertip, sticks it in and then licks it off.

'That's unsanitary.' Rosie smiles again.

'It's okay. I've had my shots.'

Lorraine, the head waitress, comes over, sits down next
to Rosie, takes Joe's cigarettes from his shirt pocket, lights
one up and says hello. Joe's been in five or six times in the
three years Rosie's been working there. When he and
Lorraine met they took to each other immediately. A smile
always comes over her face when Joe walks in.

She's in her mid-fifties but still slim and has a tight, fast
way of moving. She can be doing a dozen things at once
and keep tabs on all of them. She keeps a lit cigarette
burning in at least five ashtrays in different parts of the
restaurant. That way, whenever she touches down at any
of the waitress stations, the kitchen or behind the cash
register, there's always one waiting for her. She smokes the
100's because they last longer. Joe once saw a man reach up
her skirt as she bent down to set his plate in front of him.
She didn't stop what she was doing. She filled his coffee,
asked if he wanted anything else, wrote out his check and
then, in the same matter-of-fact tone of voice, told him that
if he ever did that again she'd cut his throat. Sometimes
Joe'd come in just to see her.

'How ya doin?' she asks Joe. 'Take the day off?'

'Yup.' He's glad to see her but at the moment has

nothing more to say.

'Hey. You two are goin on vacation next week. We're sure gonna miss Rosie around here.'

Joe looks at Rosie. Lorraine realizes that she sat down in the middle of something, gets up, says she has work to do and heads for the kitchen. On her next trip by she sets a coffee cup in front of Joe and fills it.

'Is it the vacation?' Joe asks Rosie. 'Did I screw it up?'
She doesn't answer.

'Rosie... Is that why ya just left last night and didn't leave a note or anything? Is that it?'

'I guess.'

'Did I screw it up?'

'We can still go... If ya want to.'

'Do *you*?'

'If you do.'

'Is that what was bothering ya? I want ta know.'

'I guess. I don't know.'

'Does Iris want me ta go?'

'You'll haveta behave.'

'Okay. Only I can't believe they really want me ta go.'

'I want you ta try an like em. They're my friends.'

'Yeah...'

'Yeah?' She caps the last pourer. Then begins setting them on a tray.

'Yeah. Only how could I like em if they don't like me... ROSIE...'

'SSSH, you're beginning ta shout.'

'Rosie...' Now quieter, 'How could ya like people like that?'

'I should like Joe Flushing Avenue?'

She gets up, walks to the beginning of her section and sets the sugar pourers on the ends of each table. She forms a group with one pourer, the salt and pepper shakers and the mustard and ketchup squeeze bottles. She draws them all together between her palms and fingers, like a pool player racking balls. Joe, clumsy, out of place, follows her along.

'No, ya don't have ta like Joe Flushing Avenue, only . . .'

'They're *my* friends. They like me. Just cause they don't hang out an drink beer, that doesn't mean I can't like em.'

'I know, I know, only Rosie . . . only . . . I don't know . . .'

'What?'

'Ya seem different.'

Lorraine floats by and stops at the table with a coffee pot, hovering over Joe's cup.

'Want more?'

'Please.'

'How do ya mean, different?' Rosie asks.

They sit down again.

'I don't know. Ya been spendin so much time with them. Sometimes ya seem like you're on their side instead a mine. I don't know, Rosie. What's goin on?'

'There are things I like ta do with them. I want you ta be there too only you'd rather hang out at Mary's. An if ya do come you never talk.'

'But I'm your husband.'

'An ya spend most of your time with *your* friends. Can't ya understand? There are things *I* want.'

'Like what. What do ya want?'

'More than just ta sunbathe in the backyard or sit at home while you're out at Mary's. Maybe I want ta finish school. Maybe even go to graduate school.'

'Like Iris.'

'Yeah.' She looks at Joe. 'Like Iris.'

He looks around the table, at its Formica pattern with little colored boomerangs. He keeps changing his focus so that sometimes it looks like the white was there first and the boomerangs were laid on top and sometimes it looks like the boomerangs were there first and the white was filled in inside and around them.

'Didja hear me?' she says.

'Yeah...' He looks up. 'WHO'S STOPPIN YA?'

'Quiet, you're yellin again.'

'I'm not yellin.'

'You *are* yelling,' from Lorraine, who's standing next to Rosie. 'I hate to interrupt, but Rosie...' She points to the clock over the cash register. 'It's a quarter to.'

'Oh shit,' Rosie says. 'I gotta finish setting up... Joe, lunches'll be coming in.'

'Okay, I'll see ya later.'

Lorraine gives Joe a peck on the cheek, scoops up his coffee cup and drops it into a bus box on her way into the kitchen.

'Joe,' Rosie says, 'I'll see you later. Okay?'

'Yeah.'

He walks out the door and heads straight for the A train. He wants to be out of downtown Manhattan before the office buildings let out their workers for lunch. In that area at twelve noon, when the doors open it's like unscrewing the valve on an inner tube, only the buildings don't shrink and flatten out like tires.

He doesn't like what he's feeling. Things are happening that he has no control over. Rosie is changing. He might even be losing her. *Nah, we've had fights before.* He tries to reduce the feeling, but he can't shake it off. She wants him to change somehow, but he can't. She knew who she was marrying. Now she wants a college professor. *Fuck it, she can go to school if she wants. We can afford it. She can even quit her job if she wants to. We've had fights before. We can beat this thing, whatever it is, that's comin between us.*

They were sure they'd have a better marriage than their parents. On either side. During the weeks before their wedding they spoke about it almost every time they were together. A marriage license and time would not change the way they related to each other. They were sure. Rosie's parents opposed the marriage but theirs was no example. In fact, their not wanting Rosie to marry Joe was the first thing they'd agreed upon in ten years. They hadn't slept together for longer.

Joe used to do a little routine about his parents. He'd do it in comic voices. He called it 'Saturday Night,' and it was an imitation of their conversations. He and Rosie'd be out walking, having dinner, riding on a bus, and Joe'd say to her, 'Ya ready for a big Saturday Night?' and Rosie'd laugh.

'Jimmy, turn up Jackie Gleason, willya? I'm washin my hair inna sink and I can't hear with the water runnin.'

'WHAT? I can't hear ya. The water's runnin.'

'TURN UP THE TV.'

'Carmen, while you're in there take out the gnocchi and let em defrost, willya? Last Sunday they was cold inna middle an I hate gnocchi that's cold inna middle.'

'If ya don't like my cookin ya can eat out.'

(In response, as Jimmy, he'd let out a belch.)

'Jimmy are you drinkin beer on my coffee table? . . . Are you usin a coaster?'

'Carmen, do me a favor . . . '

'Are you usin a coaster?'

'While ya got ya head inna sink, why don't ya drown yourself.'

They could beat this easy. There was no strain, no boredom. They were wiser, worldlier, in love, younger. A piece of cake.

He feels a need for her. He hasn't felt this in a long time and he doesn't like it. It makes him feel weak and he doesn't like feeling weak.

When he gets home he tries to take a nap, but he can't fall asleep even though he barely slept the night before. He goes into the living room and turns on the TV. *Hollywood Squares*. The announcer asks a pretty schoolteacherly young woman if she agrees with Paul Lynde's answer to this question: What do you call someone who is half European and half Asian.

'A waiter' is his answer.

Everyone laughs.

The young woman disagrees.

Joe doesn't get it. He turns off the TV. It's a dumb fuckin show anyway.

16

JOE IS JUST WALKING IN from the grocery store when Joe
Flushing Avenue calls to find out why he called in sick. Joe
tells him he just didn't feel like coming in.

'Ya know, just cause they give ya eight sick days, that
doesn't mean ya have ta take em all.'

'What time is it anyway?' Joe's looking into the
refrigerator as he talks and it just occurred to him that
Rosie should be home soon. He takes a pack of Marlboros
out of the bag and throws it on the kitchen table, then a
bottle of Pepsi and a half-pound package of Genoa salami,
which he unwraps and takes a slice from before putting it
into the Tupperware cold-cut box on the top shelf.

'Four. I'm callin from the office. Ya know they keep a
count. You should be careful.'

'If they gave me three hundred and sixty I'd take all of
em.'

'What is this, the sixth? The seventh?'

'I don't know. Ask them, they keep count.'

'Anyway, I called ta find out if ya wanted ta visit Sonny tomorrow. We can punch out at three and take the two hours as personal time.'

'Look whose talking about time off.'

'Yeah, but this is legal. Ya gonna come or not? I'll put in for the time now.'

'Sure, why not.'

Their contract allows them two days worth of personal time per year and hospital visits are one of the things you can use it for. Other uses for personal time, as specified in the *Collective Bargaining Agreement Between Brooklyn/Queens Water Resources and Its Employees*, are as follows: Visits to of Children's Teachers, Children's Needs, Legal Matters, Funerals, and, *only when absolutely necessary*, Other Unavoidable Personal Business, which has come to be interpreted as hangovers and/or Fridays.

They know the personal time will be easy to get, even after Joe's sick day, because Joe Flushing Avenue has a lot of seniority and also because their sector is almost finished. They just have to clean up the *not homes* and *no accesses*. They can easily have that done by the day after tomorrow, which is Friday, Joe's last day before vacation. Afterwards, hopefully, he will not see South Ozone Park for at least another year.

'Didja have a talk with Rosie? Is that why ya took the day off? Didja do what I said?'

'I forgot what ya said.'

'Tell her ta stop hangin around with that smartass friend a hers. Remember?'

'Yeah.'

'A married woman can't run around pullin shit like that. She can't do what *she* wants... a married woman's gotta do what *you* want.'

Rosie's parents had told her that if she married Joe she'd never be able to do the things she wanted. They told her this several times but, like everything else they said, it went in one ear, out the other and off into space. By now, traveling at the speed of sound, these words should be passing Mars, which is where, Joe still believes, they should be. He wonders if Rosie still does. Yeah... she must. Everybody's got something to say, her parents, Joe Flushing Avenue. It's all a hundred percent bullshit.

'Well, didja do it?'

'Do what?'

'Talk ta Rosie.'

'Uh uh. I took the day off cause I wasn't in the mood ta spend it walkin around in people's basements... '

He was going to add, 'An listenin to your bullshit for eight hours,' but instead he just said that he was tired, good-bye, and hung up.

At dinner Rosie is pensive and much quieter than usual. Joe tells her she should go back to college if she really wants to. She could even quit her job. They can afford it. If she wants to. He doesn't want her to think he's standing in her way.

She tells him she will and she's glad he gave it some thought. It's too late for the fall semester, but she could start in February.

He thought this would make her happy, his wanting her to go back to school, but she's still quiet and uncommunicative. Her parents, Joe Flushing Avenue, Iris, anything any of them have to say is a hundred percent bullshit.

After dinner they sit in the living room, Joe, lying in front of the TV, Rosie sitting on the couch, her legs curled under her, reading *Tropic of Cancer*. He lies there pretending he's not aware of the silence. Usually he isn't aware of the weight of the silences that occur between them. Usually he instigates them. But Rosie isn't just not talking, she's thinking. Maybe, in the past, she has often become this deeply absorbed in her thoughts. If so, he never noticed. It disturbs him.

He asks her about Iris and Roger, and she tells him that she called them that afternoon. They're going up on Friday and expecting Joe and Rosie on Monday.

'There's a bus in the morning.'

'Are you sure they want me ta come?' he asks her.

'Yeah. Iris said it would be fine.'

'We don't have ta spend all our time with em, right? . . . Rosie? We can go fishin.'

'Wrong. We're their guests. We have some responsibilities.'

'Yeah, you're right. We'll bring em a bottle of wine and a box of assorted pastries. Then we'll go fishin.'

Rosie doesn't find him all that funny. She goes back to her book.

A little while later she gets up and goes into the bedroom. Joe shouts in to her that it's only 9:30. She shouts back that she's not sleeping, she's reading.

When the ten o'clock news comes on, Joe turns off the TV, takes a shower and slides into bed next to Rosie.

She's no longer reading, she's lying on her back with the open book on her chest.

He asks her if she wants him to turn off the air conditioner, and she tells him not to unless he's ready to go to sleep. She closes the book and lays it on the night table. Then lies back and closes her eyes. No part of her is touching Joe. This is a conscious act and she is quietly tense with the effort.

'Didja notice how much better it works since I put in the new filter?'

'Yeah,' she says.

'An it uses less electricity too . . . Rosie?'

'What?'

'What the hell is it? So I got a little pissed at ya friend Iris. Big deal.'

'Joe?'

'What?'

'Do you think our marriage is working?'

'Of course. Yeah. It's workin... why?' He turns to Rosie.

'I don't know. We never do anything together. We never have fun anymore. We never even talk.'

'Whaddaya mean?' He's beginning to wish he had stayed inside, watching TV. 'We're talkin now.'

'Yeah, but it's not the same. I mean the rest of the time. It's like we don't have stuff we want ta say ta each other.'

'Joe is thinking, then suddenly jumps out of bed and looks at Rosie.

'It's Iris, that bitch! What's she been tellin ya?'

'Nothing.'

'*Bullshit!*' He walks around the bed, picks up his cigarettes, lights one. 'That bitch's been tellin ya you're too good for me. Am I right? I'm holding ya back. Right?'

'Wrong.' Rosie's sitting up now. 'She hasn't said anything. This is between you and me.'

'Bullshit! That's why you're behavin so weird lately. Fine...'

'Joe...'

'Fine. Pack up ya shit an move in with her... only she'll never be able ta wear your bathin suits. Uh uh. Ya know what she looks like? She looks like an overstuffed sausage.'

He walks into the bathroom, turns on the light, throws his cigarette into the toilet, turns it off, walks back into the bedroom.

'Fine. See what I care.'

'Joe, we haveta talk about this. You haveta listen.'

'I'm listenin fine.' He lights another cigarette. 'Move in with her. Every night the two a yas can go to another dumb fuckin movie. And go ta college for the rest of ya lives. An every place ya live ya can paint the radiator yellow. Jesus, that yellow radiator. *That's* the cat's fuckin meow... '

He walks into the living room, turns on the TV and sits for a minute.

Rosie lies down again and listens. He gets up, walks around and then walks into the kitchen. She doesn't look at him.

She hears him open the refrigerator, uncap a beer and go back into the living room. A minute later he's back in the bedroom for cigarettes. She pretends she is asleep.

She will not try to talk to him. In a few minutes he gets another beer and goes back into the living room. She hears the theme from *The Odd Couple*. She is crying. He will not change.

17

JOE AND JOE FLUSHING AVENUE are sitting in the lobby of Jamaica Hospital. The hospital allows each patient only five visitors at a time, and right now Mary, Sonny's two brothers and their wives are up in his room. They issue each visitor a big plastic-coated pass with the patient's name and room number on it. If you don't have one, or if you're not wearing a white jacket with a stethoscope poking out of the side pocket, the guards at the elevators won't let you pass.

They left South Ozone Park at 2:30, punched out at 3:00 and then drove over in Joe Flushing Avenue's Belair.

They're sitting in a row of attached, hard plastic seats that come in four colors and repeat the same pattern over and over: yellow, blue, orange, green. Joe remembers seeing the same exact pattern of colors on a set of bars worn by a major he met in Saigon. He was sitting in a bar at the time, alone and thoroughly smashed. The major sat on the empty stool next to his and Joe leaned over and told him

that the bar they were in was okay but the bars he was
wearing were dazzling. The major was drunk enough at
the time to think Joe was funny and bought him a drink.
Joe can't remember for sure, but he thinks the bars meant
the guy was a big wheel in antipersonnel artillery back in
Korea.

Joe's flipping through a week-old copy of *People*
magazine. Joe Flushing Avenue periodically gets up, walks
over to the reception desk and tries to start a conversation
with the nurse on duty. The lobby is filled with friends and
families waiting for other visitors to come down and turn in
their passes. Also, nurses and orderlies on their way to or
from somewhere and children running all over the place. A
little girl runs over Joe Flushing Avenue's feet with her big-
wheel tricycle when she tries to imagine a tunnel between
his leaning body and the reception desk. At the time he was
telling the nurse that she was pretty enough to be a
stewardess if she wanted to be.

An old man, with his hat in his hands and the dark,
wrinkled skin of a European peasant, is standing next to a
pillar a few feet from where Joe's sitting. He looks very lost.
Joe walks over and asks him if he can be of some help. He
offers him his seat.

'No thanks. I stand.'

'Ya sure ya don't need any help?'

'No. They tell me to stand right here,' and he points to
the floor at his feet. Then he turns forward again. He's
waiting.

'Okay,' Joe says.

He sits down again and goes back to his magazine. His
eye is caught by a photo of Cher. She is kneeling like a cat,
facing the camera, her long brown hair touching the floor.
He reads the caption, whcih says that she planned to cut off
all her hair. Then in smaller print it goes on to say that she
flew some famous hairdresser all the way in from Paris,

then at the last minute changed her mind.

Mary's sitting next to Sonny's bed, spoon-feeding him some kind of pudding, when they walk in. Both of his brothers and their wives have left. Joe Flushing Avenue had seen him last week, but his appearance is a complete surprise to Joe. You can see the outline of his shrunken body under the blanket. He is half the size he was the last time Joe saw him. His head seems enormous in comparison. He takes in mouthfuls of pudding as Mary offers them, unable to lift his hands, barely able to keep his head erect.

He says hello to Joe and Joe Flushing Avenue. The last few times Joe'd seen him, over two years ago, he didn't even say that much. He'd pass him occasionally on the street or see him on his way in or out of Mary's, and those times, if somebody was screaming rape, fire and murder, let alone his name, he wouldn't have looked up.

'How ya doin?' Joe Flushing Avenue walks over to him, rubs his hair. 'Ya looking better today.'

'Bullshit.'

He turns his head towards Joe.

'Hey Joey. How ya doin?' He stops for a second and swallows. 'Hey, ya sure got big since ya useta sneak sips outta my beer at those card games. Remember?'

'Sure do. It's great ta see ya.'

'Ya mean what's left a me.'

'Stop it, Sonny,' Mary says. She puts the spoon back into the bowl on the rolling tray that slides over the bed, wipes his mouth and sits back, her hands in her lap. 'Joe didn't come ta hear that.'

Joe Flushing Avenue walks over to Mary's side of the bed, pulls up a chair and sits.

'Didn't ya go inta the army?' Sonny asks Joe. 'When didja get out?'

Somewhere he had misplaced ten years.

'A while ago, Sonny. I'm workin with Joe Flushing Avenue now.'

'Oh yeah, I remember. Hey Joey. Don't lissen ta anything he tella ya.' Then, in a whisper, 'He'll get ya in trouble.'

'I won't.' Joe smiles.

A nurse walks in, picks up the pudding bowl and asks Sonny if he's done.

'Not quite, honey.' He winks. 'Just slide in here next ta me an I'll show ya.'

Joe Flushing Avenue laughs. The nurse smiles, rolls back the tray and leaves with the bowl. Then another nurse walks in, wheeling a cart with rows of little paper cups on it. She takes one with three pills in it and, holding the back of Sonny's head with one hand, pours them into his mouth. Then she lifts another cup to his lips. This one with water.

The whole time Joe Flushing Avenue is watching her from behind, nodding up and down slowly, following her white-stockinged legs up to where they meet the hem of her dress and then back down again. Mary's just sitting there, her hands in her lap, still holding the napkin she used to wipe Sonny's mouth.

When the nurse leaves, Joe Flushing Avenue tells Sonny that they sure got some good-looking nurses in this joint.

Sonny smiles, then he turns his eyes back to Joe.

'Remember what I told ya. He'll get ya in trouble.' In a little while Sonny falls asleep. Mary arranges his blanket, then tells them she has to go. It's time to open up.

'He'll sleep for a while now. One a the pills they give him makes him sleep.'

After she leaves they sit there watching Sonny.

'What's happening with you an Rosie?' Joe Flushing Avenue asks.

'Nothin.'

'Ya still goin upstate ta visit her friend, what's her name,

Irene?'

'Iris.'

'Yeah. Ya still goin?'

'I don't know.'

'Why don't ya tell Rosie ya not goin an that's that.'

'Stay out of it.'

'No, lissen. Then bring her someplace nice. Maybe that place up in the Catskills ya went ta when ya got married.'

Joe doesn't answer. He just watches Sonny.

They both just sit there for a while. Not talking. Just watching Sonny sleep. Then Joe Flushing Avenue asks if Joe knew that Sonny's real name was also Joe.

'No,' Joe says. 'Really?'

'That's right. *Joseph.* We go back a long way me an Sonny. They called him Sonny on account a his father's name also bein Joseph.'

The nurse who took away the pudding bowl walks back in. She checks on Sonny, then gives them a bland, professional-nurse-smile on the way out.

'I like the other one better,' Joe Flushing Avenue says, 'but if this one wants ta, she can sleep with me too... Anyway,' he goes on, 'like I was sayin, we go back a long way.'

'From before the war?' Joe asks. He knows they had been in the service together.

'We grew up together, on Navy Street. We both went ta St. Michael's. Then, when we were teenagers the Navy Yard started expandin, so we all had ta move. His family went ta Ridgewood. We went ta Flushing Avenue. He was the first one ta call me Joe Flushing Avenue. Didja know that?'

'Uh uh.'

'Yeah, but that was later.'

'In the navy?'

'Yeah. When the war started we joined up together.

They put us both in the galley. Every time somebody said, hey Joe, wash out this pot, or hey Joe, eighty-six this garbage, we'd both come runnin. After a while I realized if I pretended I didn't hear nothin, he'd do it anyway. Ya know what I'm sayin?'

'Yeah.'

'Anyway, he figures it out, so one day he goes up ta the CPO an says, lissen, from now on call that slob Joe Flushing Avenue. I'm tired a doin his work!' He laughs quietly now. He's happy that Joe's listening.

'By the end a the war he's second cook and I'm still scrubbin pots so big I had ta climb inside em.'

A man sticks his head in the door and asks if they know where room 320 is. He's about Joe's age, black and wearing a mailman's uniform. He's also carrying the pith helmet they sometimes wear in the summer. Joe Flushing Avenue shrugs. Joe tells him it's probably further down the hall since this is 307.

Joe's beginning to get antsy. He's not sure what time it is but he's sure it's almost dinnertime. He wants to go home, have it out with Rosie and get it over with. *What the hell*, he tells himself, they've had fights before. The problems between him and Rosie are easier to fit into this kind of perspective now, with only a small part of his mind on the intensity and confusion, watching Sonny, near death, sleeping now so peacefully.

Joe Flushing Avenue continues:

'Right after we come home, Mary and Sonny get married and he gets a job in this Italian restaurant in the city. That's when I started workin with Water Resources. In those days we useta go out all the time. We were a team, tearin off pieces all over the city. Then one day he says he's gotta stop cause Mary don't like it. I'm getting him in trouble, he says. Whaddya mean? I tell em, but he says I can't call no more cause Mary don't like it. Anyway we end up having this big fight about it... '

Joe gets up and looks for a clock down the hall.

'Go on. I'm listening.'

'Around this time. This musta been forty-eight, forty-nine, yeah, forty-nine, he gets a job in this resort up in Lake George, an he an Mary move up there. By the time he moves back he's drinkin like a fish, the Dodgers are in Los Angeles and we're friends again.'

They decide it's time to go. It's been an hour since Sonny fell asleep.

On their way to the elevator they pass room 320 and Joe looks in at the mailman's family. Two little girls, about five and eight, two women, one of whom is probably his wife, all sitting around a bed in which an older woman is sitting up and eating dinner. They seem happy. Whatever she is in for, she'll be going home. Joe recognizes the younger of the two girls as the one who ran over Joe Flushing Avenue's feet in the waiting room.

When they turn in their passes Joe Flushing Avenue takes one last shot at the reception nurse. He asks her why she's wasting her life stuck behind that desk when she could be flying around the world with TWA. She tells him she'd like to go out with him, only her husband, who just finished a ten-year stretch for manslaughter, would probably like him even less than she does.

After Joe Flushing Avenue drops him off Joe sits on the front stoop for a while. It's almost six and Rosie must be home and he's not yet ready to go upstairs. Things don't seem so comprehensible anymore now that he's home.

This morning he left before she woke up. He wishes the whole thing were over and things were back to normal. Just because he yelled at her friend Iris. He restrained himself for five-fuckin-years. How come he's the only one not allowed to have opinions? That's what *he* wants to know.

Stacia Heally is sitting on the stoop directly across from Joe. She's listening to a portable radio and doing her nails. He watches her.

He's afraid anything he might say to Rosie will make matters worse. He wishes the whole thing were over.

There have been periods in his life where nothing seemed to happen for long stretches of time but this isn't one of them. Things are beginning to happen fast. There's so much he still doesn't understand. He's not sure what she wants in general. A lot more will have to happen before his life plateaus again. He wishes he were past it all, resting in a long period of sameness.

He looks over at Stacia, sitting there, no older than sixteen, at peace, the air around her as empty as her thoughts. There's nothing on its way from who-knows-where to fuck up her life. No problems. Not for a long time and she knows it.

At six o'clock she turns the dial of her radio until she finds a station without news. She blows each nail when she finishes it, then holds her hand at arm's length to see it from a distance, as if she were someone else, and admires her work.

18

STACIA HEALLY is finished. She picks up the white-tipped bottle of nail polish and holds it loosely in her hand. Then she bends down again, in a deep knee bend, and picks up the portable radio between her elbow and side, like a bird closing its wing. With just the tips of the fingers of her other hand she opens the screen door and slips inside.

Joe remembers the list of options he wrote down for Dr. Seidman at the VA Hospital five years ago. Number 5 is beginning to look a lot better. *Sittin on the dock of the bay watchin the ti-ime ro-oll away.*

Maybe the right way to deal with all this shit is to walk away from it — permanently. It would have to be the real thing. Not just walking out of your life for a while and haunting somebody's basement like it was a travel book. But to be a real option it would have to be a possible one — not one of the half-serious, childish impossibilities he wrote down five years ago. At the time he didn't know what Dr. Seidman meant by "really unhappy."

He needs a viable alternative, one with a crossable gap

between where *it* is and where *he* is now.

Dougie Lewis, one of the guys who hangs out in Mary's, spends his winter in Aspen, Colorado, where he's a cook in a ski lodge. He works from Halloween to Easter. Every year he shows up right after Easter and tells everybody he just rose up from the dead. During the summer he lives with his mother and collects unemployment. If Joe left for a job like that, he *wouldn't* come back. It would be the first stop on a trip anywhere.

Dougie tells him they have a big turnover. Maybe a third of the people come back from the year before. They don't just hire in the kitchen either. There's seasonal work in the ski shop, and for drivers and maintenance as well. He could get him a job easy.

That's an option with a possibility. If the shit got impossible he'd have a winter's head start. From there he could try somewhere else. He'll have a talk with Dougie next time he sees him.

In spring he could make it the rest of the way to the *Bay*. He's got his own will. Shit. *Just in case.* If this shit gets too thick he's covered.

At this time of year, the leaves on the Norway maples and sycamores that line 109th Street and many of Richmond Hill's side streets are at their thickest and darkest green. If you're driving down the block and look up, you often can't see the sky. It's like driving through a tunnel of leaves. In deep summer the trees give a foreign, almost exotic look to the streets. They offer some relief to the rows of picture windows and bright shingles and light gray or red synthetic stone facings that began to cover all the house fronts in the early sixties. At that time the fathers of Richmond Hill were in their forties, had paid off most of their mortgages and could now not only afford to pay their kids' dentist bills and buy washing machines for their wives, but could also modernize their homes so they'd look like the newer, larger ones out in the real suburbs.

Around this time *The Honeymooners* went off the air because the parents of Richmond Hill lost interest in Ralph and Alice Cramden. Riley and Madge and Junior were out too. Now your father was Ward Cleaver. And if you were eleven or twelve, standing in front of your little lawn and your picture window, you were The Beaver. It was almost the same. Even if your school was integrated. Even if your brother Wally and Eddie Haskell got a little drunk the night before and threw a bubble-gum machine through the window of Dugan's grocery store on the corner.

When Joe walks in, the table is set and dinner is ready. Rosie doesn't seem as angry or as cold or, in any visible way, as upset as he was sure she would be. When he walks in she smiles and asks about Sonny. Joe describes his condition and Rosie says that it's a shame.

She takes a salad out of the refrigerator, then a plate of fried-chicken cutlets and sits down. Then she says, oh, the lemons, gets up, goes back to the refrigerator and comes back with a saucer of sliced lemons. Joe doesn't start eating. He just watches her.

'Joe,' she finally says, 'we haveta talk, or rather *I* haveta talk. An this time you haveta listen.' She is not angry. She's direct and firm.

Joe agrees. She will put her foot down and he won't try to lift it.

She tells him that their life together hasn't resembled a marriage for a long time. They've stopped communicating the way people are supposed to. He spends nearly all of his free time at Mary's... or wherever. She doesn't know anymore and she's stopped asking. She has also found things to occupy her time and they are things *she* likes.

'You understand so far?' she asks.

'Yeah Rosie.' He understands that he's not happy either but he doesn't know of many marriages that are much different. In fact, he's not sure how one is supposed to *be* married. Not from here he doesn't, not from the middle of their present relationship. He thinks this but doesn't tell Rosie.

'If, just ta be happy, we haveta spend all our time in different places, what's the point of bein married in the first place?'

She looks at Joe. He half shrugs, half nods.

'It sems ta me that we have three choices. Either we get divorced now... '

'*What?*'

'Wait. You agreed ta listen.'

'All right.'

'The second choice is ta go on like we've been an either kill each other or get a divorce within a year. And the third is ta work very hard, both of us, an try ta make this relationship a marriage again. That means doing things together. You'll have ta respect *my* wishes too.'

Joe is thinking that it would be easy if Iris and Roger weren't included in them.

'I thought our relationship would grow an we'd somehow be able ta feel it... that it would show. We'd be in a bigger place, maybe have different things around us, maybe a house of our own... I don't know... feel settled.'

'Like my parents were settled?'

'No. But, Jesus, we're married five years an we can't even sit across a table from each other.'

'We're sittin now.'

'Yeah, we're sittin *now*... '

'I'm sorry, Rosie. You're right.'

'I don't know what a marriage is supposed ta be but I know our problems are for real, an we haveta talk about em when they come up an I mean for real. No more shuttin up like a clam or screamin when something upsets you. I want a future. But we can't have one if we don't get along in the present.'

'Who said that?' Joe asks. 'That last thing?'

'I did. Why?'

'Oh. I thought it mighta been that guy, Arthur Miller.'

'No, it was me. An I think you mean Henry Miller.'

'Yeah.'

'Have you been listening?'

'Yeah, Rosie. I have.'

'I want ya to think about it for a while. Go inside or something. Don't just say something. Think about it.'

He goes inside and sits on the couch. He can't find anything to think about. He doesn't want to lose Rosie.

He goes back into the kitchen. Rosie's washing the dishes. He walks up behind her, slips his hands under her blouse and lowers his head onto her shoulder.

'I'm sorry I got upset an everything last night, Rosie. It surprised me too. Ya know I don't want ta hurt ya.'

She doesn't answer. She's crying. She keeps washing the dishes.

Joe asks her why she's crying and she says that she wonders what difference it will make in the long run — what they really want.

'Don't worry,' he tells her. 'It'll work out. I'll try. I promise.'

He turns her around. She keeps her arms out because they're dripping with suds. Then she comes into his arms. She is still crying and she gets soapsuds all over his hair and the back of his neck.

He asks her if she uses the kind they show on TV.

'Ya know, the kind that softens your skin.'

'Yeah,' she says, 'but I wonder if anything can soften your head.'

19

WHILE ROSIE'S PACKING, Joe walks over to Wise Drugs on Jamaica Avenue to pick up some things they'll need for the trip. She wants suntan lotion with coconut oil and insect repellent. Joe throws in a carton of Marlboros.

He'll be polite to Iris and Roger as long as they're polite to him. That's the arrangement they agreed upon.

Yesterday was their last day in South Ozone Park. With any luck he won't see those basements for another year. Maybe never. A year is a long time. By then Mrs. Voletsky's son might have given up the accordion and become a juvenile delinquent who assaults other thirteen-year-olds and steals their lunch money. Or, in that time, he becomes so good that they'll make him the youngest accordionist on the Lawrence Welk show. A lot can happen. By then Joe might be sandblasting skyscrapers for a living.

He walks past the Q & T Diner. Mr. Dugan is standing out front, his hands in his pockets, watching the traffic, whistling. He is standing about ten feet farther down the avenue from where he stood last month, on the morning Joe met Denise on her way to work. It was about the same time of day, but by now, August 17, the sun is much lower and the awning's shadow cools the pavement more than ten feet beyond itself.

It feels like a lot more than a month ago since he met Denise. He had been really moved by that night with her but he quickly made it a part of his past. She was really crazy with her poems and her accent like a TV news reporter. The blackout has completely disappeared from newspapers and television. For two weeks it was all you heard about. No one even talks about it anymore. Almost like it never happened.

But there's one moment that comes back to him often, and easily. The two of them lying against the concrete wall, her leg slipped over his, the complete, empty darkness. He hadn't felt that calm in years and hasn't since. He still has the rumpled piece of paper with her phone number on it in his wallet. But when you're married you have to be careful. You don't shit where you eat. Besides, she was into that weird 'hunter' business. He could never get into that kind of crap.

Joe nods to Mr. Dugan, who still doesn't recognize him, which makes sense since he didn't recognize him a month ago, and now it's another month farther away from Joe's childhood years, which is when he last really knew him.

He never seems to whistle those tunes. Just little snatches of things, sweet, upbeat phrases that invoke film images of the Andrew Sisters, sailors tap-dancing on the deck of a ship, Rita Hayworth in a bathing suit, the cocked, angular hats of the forties.

Richie Heally, the eldest of Stacia's four brothers, is washing his Firebird. Richie's about two years older than Joe. He's a policeman. He got married a year ago, but he and his wife still live with his parents.

Joe tells him that he and Rosie are going on vacation. To help explain he opens the paper bag and shows Richie the plastic bottle of suntan oil.

'Where ya goin?' Richie asks.

'Upstate. We have friends.' Joe frowns at the word 'friends'. Then he reminds himself that it's a beautiful day and that they'll have over a week's vacation left when they come back.

Earlier, when he and Rosie were having their coffee, he noticed that the *Sell By* date on the milk container was the day they'd be coming home. Five days isn't long. It takes longer than that for milk to go sour.

Richie tells Joe that last week he and Vicki paid the down payment on their own house.

'It's right up the block. You remember the Caputos?'

'Yeah.'

'Yeah. Since the husband died she don't wanna live there all alone. She's movin in with her sister in Jersey.'

'Makes sense,' Joe says. 'When ya movin?'

'Next week an that ain't a day too soon.' He shakes his head. 'It's time me an Vicki got our own place. We got no privacy. Man...' He leans nearer to Joe. 'We even gotta worry about the bed squeakin.'

He starts laughing. Then he bends down and picks up the hose.

Joe notices that he's wearing his off-duty pistol, a dark bulge in his white T-shirt, right in the small of his back.

Joe agrees with him, then wishes him luck.

But before leaving, Joe's curiosity gets the best of him and he asks Richie if *that*, pointing to the bulge, doesn't make him uncomfortable.

'Nah,' he says, 'ya get used to it.'

* * *

Rosie's still packing. She looks up from an opened valise and tells Joe that she can't find his bathing suit.

He tells her it's in the back of his underwear drawer but it doesn't matter because he doesn't like it.

It's the bathing suit he bought for their honeymoon and he never liked it. It's a tight blue one with a little patch on the right side with a sailfish jumping on it. He always thought it was too revealing.

Rosie tells him to take it anyway and he says no, he'd rather wear shorts or get a new one.

'Put it on,' she says.

'Why?'

'I wanna see it. Suddenly you're shy?'

He puts it on and stands there, next to the living room couch, in the tight, almost bikini-sized suit. He tells her he feels like an asshole. You can almost see the entire outline of his cock and balls.

'I feel like a ballet dancer.'

'That's you,' Rosie says. 'Nureyev The Engineer.'

'C'mon, Rosie. Be serious.'

She tells Joe it looks fine and that she likes bathing suits to fit that way. Then, with her hand, she shows him how much she likes it to fit that way.

Joe decides that maybe it isn't that bad after all. Then he tells Rosie that having discussions really isn't that hard, is it?

20

JOE AND ROSIE are the first ones to board the bus that will take them to Woodstock. They take a seat on the right side at the exact midpoint between the front and back. Joe says that in the event of a head-on collision, or if they are hit from behind, it's the safest place to be.

From outside the bus looks uncomfortably like the one in his dream. But after they settle inside and he begins to locate the distinguishing particulars that all real things have, in this case the buttons that make the seats tilt backward and the sign in the front that says, *Occupation by More Than 43 Persons Is Dangerous and Unlawful*, he becomes more at ease, assured that this is, in fact, a different bus.

Woodstock is only one of about fifteen places the bus stops at. Under the Adirondack-Trailways sign at the gate, another sign with interchangeable letters lists Kingston, Bearsville, Phoenicia, Shokan-Ashokan, Fleischmanns, Margaretville, Oneonta, Utica and about a half-dozen other places in smaller letters. Joe tells Rosie that he thinks

Shokan-Ashokan is the dumbest name for a town he'd ever heard.

That morning Joe Flushing Avenue called and Rosie answered the phone. He told her that they were lucky stiffs and to have a good time. He also told her that he'd be bartending nights for a while at Mary's and, after they came back, if she came in some night with Joe he'd buy her a drink. She thanked him and asked how Mary was holding up and he told her fine, considering. Then she handed the phone to Joe, whom he also called a lucky stiff.

'I also called ta tell ya not ta worry about Brooklyn/Queens Water Resources. I think we can get along without ya for two weeks.'

'Don't worry,' Joe told him, 'I won't.'

After the call they rushed out because Rosie was afraid they'd be late. They took the 111th Street bus to Union Turnpike and the E train to the Port Authority Bus Terminal. Even after getting their tickets and walking downstairs to the gate they were a half hour early.

A young woman walks up the aisle carrying two shiny silver overnight bags, the kind that slip inside each other when they're empty. She's wearing jeans and a T-shirt with the words *Remy Martin* written in script across the chest. She stops at the seat right in front of Joe and Rosie's. Joe watches her stretch up on her toes to throw her bags up on the baggage rack. Her thighs stretch nicely against the insides of her jeans, and her T-shirt lifts just over her belly button and exposes three inches of smooth, flat stomach. Rosie's watching the driver try to fit a ten-speed bike into the outside baggage compartment.

A minute later a guy walks up to the same seat and throws his bag on the rack. The girl slides over to the window seat and he sits down. Then he puts his arm around her and gives her a long kiss. They exchange a little tongue back and forth. Joe can see them between the headrests.

Rosie turns and sees them kissing, then Joe watching. She pokes him and laughs. As the bus fills, the couple keep on kissing like they're at a drive-in.

Joe tells Rosie he thinks he knows who they are.

'I read about em in the paper a year ago.'

'Oh yeah?' Rosie smiles. She knows this will be a good one.

'Yeah. They're from Germany. Only he's from the east side and she's from the west. He reads water meters over there.'

'Oh yeah? What does she do?'

'She glues the labels on Beck's Beer bottles.'

'Oh.'

'Anyway, one day when she's on her way ta work she stops by this hole in the wall and looks through. She does that a lot cause she's not allowed on the other side. Anyway, on this day she's lookin through and guess who's lookin through the other side?'

'Um, let me see. Fritz the cat?'

'C'mon, Rosie. Be serious.'

'Him?' She points to the guy in front of them, still kissing away.

'Yup. An they fall in love immediately. Only they could never get together cause he's from the commie side and they're not allowed ta cross over either. He tried climbin over an diggin under but he always got caught. They got strict rules about that...

'Then she began writin him messages on the insides of the labels of Beck's Beer bottles that were bein delivered over ta his side. So just ta get her messages he was goin all over the place buyin up Beck's Beer. He drank it at such an incredible rate that they had ta open a new wing just ta make enough for East Germany.'

'Didn't he get fat?'

'He blew up like a blimp. When he showed up at work his friends'd say, here comes the Hindenberg... Anyway, they decided that wasn't workin.'

'I could imagine.'

'So they decided they'd sneak outta Germany, fly to America and meet here today. Right on this bus.'

'Wow.'

'Yeah. She took a plane ta Jersey City and he flew ta Flatbush.'

'Flatbush? In Brooklyn? They don't have an airport.'

'He knew that. He parachuted.'

'I see.'

'Yeah. An they agreed ta meet on this bus an sneak away ta Shokan-Ashokan. They figured nobody in a million years'd ever come lookin for em in a place with a dumb name like that.'

'So you read all that in the paper.'

'Yup. The *Post*. An ain't we fortunate to be sittin right behind em.'

By now Romeo and Juliet have finished their make-out session. She leans over and tells him, in a whiny, nasal tone of voice, that she can't believe it's Monday.

'If this was any other Monday,' she tells Romeo, 'I'd be sitting at my typewriter yearning for my coffee break. It feels more like Saturday or Sunday or Christmas. I can't believe it's Monday.'

Joe and Rosie are laughing, quietly but hysterically. It was the last thing they expected to hear at such a momentous reunion. And not even a trace of a German accent.

The bus will arrive at 12:30 and Iris and Roger will pick them up at the station. Joe brought a fishing pole and some tackle. He has a little plastic box with a trout lure he just bought in his shirt pocket. He takes it out and plays with it. It's a little green rubber fish with a small silver spoon and three hooks at its tail. He shows Rosie how it's supposed to work.

'See. Ya cast it upstream an reel it back slow so the water makes the spoon spin and the fish kinda wobbles like it's wounded.'

He moves it in front of her so she can see the action. He spins the spoon and wiggles the fish, then, with his other hand, shows her how a trout will take it.

She isn't very impressed but she's agreed to go fishing with him once.

While the bus is squeezing through a toll lane at the entrance to the New York State Thruway, Juliet tells Romeo for at least the sixth time that she can't believe it's Monday.

'Alright, already,' he tells her in a loud voice. 'So you can't believe it's Monday. I don't fuckin care. You want me to show you a calendar?'

'I guess the honeymoon's over,' Joe tells Rosie and they burst out laughing. She tries to shush Joe but she's laughing too hard herself.

After a while Rosie takes out *Tropic of Cancer*, which she has almost finished, but she doesn't read. She watches the landscape flatten out after the Palisades and then grow slowly into the Catskills.

Joe points to the sign in the front of the bus that says they can't have more than forty-three people in it. He asks Rosie where they got the 'three' from since all the seats are in twos.

'Maybe it's the driver,' she says.

'Yeah. That's probably it.'

He feels his ears begin to pop and he asks Rosie if she feels it too.

'Not yet,' she says. 'But Iris told me that when you start feelin it in your ears you're almost there.'

He presses the button that makes the seat tilt backward.

Maybe they have a ways to go yet. Ever since he was in the service his ears have been sensitive. Sometimes they pop for no reason at all. Even when he's down in a basement.

part three

October 31–November 6

21

JOE'S ON HIS WAY downstairs to answer the door when the bell rings for the third time. He yells to whoever is doing the ringing to keep his shirt on.

He opens the door and sees a boy, maybe eight years old, dressed as a hobo and holding the hand of a little, white-sheeted ghost with both her eyes and her nose and mouth peeking through one of the eyeholes. It's six o'clock and already dark. It was a clear day and it's becoming a clear night. The air carries the smell of burning leaves — not from a specific direction — but as one of its component elements. It's the old people, or a few of them, say one every four square blocks or so, who no one has yet told that somewhere back in the fifties it became illegal to burn leaves in the streets.

On 109th Street the leaves have been swept into the gutters and the cars parked along the curbs are hubcap-deep in them.

'Trick-a-treat,' the hobo says.

He's carrying a shopping bag with the words *Thank You For Shopping Woolworth's* on its side. Along with his raggy patched shirt and pants he's wearing a rubber Groucho Marx mask with glasses and a big nose.

'Who are ya supposed ta be?' Joe asks.

'A bum,' he answers.

'An I'm a ghost,' the ghost tells him.

'Well, hold on a minute,' Joe says and runs back upstairs.

When he comes back down he's got a package of Oreos.

The hobo's shopping bag is about one-third full of chocolate bars, hard candy, bubble gum, orange wax harmonicas, apples and a few dollars' worth of loose nickels, dimes and pennies. The ghost has a hollow plastic pumpkin with a wire handle, like a pail's, about half full of the same loot.

He gives them each a handful of Oreos.

The hobo looks at Joe like he just bought a ten-cent pretzel with a twenty-dollar bill and didn't get his change.

'That's it,' Joe tells him.

He gives Joe a look of disbelief. Then he takes the little ghost's hand, shakes his head and leads her down the stoop, which she can only take one step at a time.

When he gets back to the sidewalk he turns to Joe and yells, 'What a gyp!'

'Get a fuckin job!' Joe yells back and slams the door.

It was Rosie who used to worry about Halloween. She'd buy those big packs of candy bars they sell in the A & P and little wax flutes and soda bottles with syrup inside. She kept them in a fishbowl downstairs by the front door. She enjoyed answering the door and doling out the candy. She liked to do things like pretend the little ghost was really scary or ask the hobo if he needed a dime for a cup of coffee.

But four weeks ago, yesterday, she announced at dinner that she was moving in with Linda and Frank.

'Just for a while,' she said. 'We have to try something else. I've made up my mind.'

Joe just looked at her when she said it.

She looked at her plate, waiting.

'What's that gonna do?' he asked her.

He got up and paced around the table. Rosie watched him, her cheek leaning into her hand.

'WHAT'S THAT GONNA DO?'

'I've made up my mind. It's the best thing for us both.'

'Oh, you've made up ya mind.' He was hissing with anger. 'An ya want a divorce.'

'Not a divorce. No. Just ta see what it's like ta live separately for a while. Then we'll decide.'

'How long you been plannin this?'

'I've thought about it.'

'How long?'

'Months. Maybe the whole last year.'

'An ya never told me?'

'I wanted to. You're hard ta talk to. I was scared. I wanted ta tell ya the night we had that fight. The night after ya came in an saw me at work.'

'Why didn't ya?'

'I was scared.'

'Of me?'

'Of you, of myself. . . of really doin it. But Joe, I know it's the best thing. Maybe it can work out. Maybe it can't. I don't know. But we haveta try this. Ta see.'

For a month before this they were constantly fighting. When they got back from Iris and Roger's he told Rosie he never wanted to see those assholes again. He had tried. He wouldn't discuss it.

After that they fought about everything *but* Iris and Roger. Rosie began spending even more time with Iris. Some nights Joe'd go out right from work and not come home until after Rosie was asleep. Some nights she'd come home after he did.

One night Rosie made green spinach macaroni instead of the white kind. Joe told her he didn't like it and she said it was better for them, less starch and not as fattening.

'Is this the kind ya friend Iris eats?' he asked.

'If ya want ta know, *yes*.'

He threw it in the sink and went out.

If she came home with a new blouse or earrings or a new book it would drive him up the wall. If she came in looking satisfied, looking as if she had a good time somewhere else where the air was better, he couldn't help saying something that would cause a fight. He began to see everything she did as another wedge she was driving between them.

She started wearing her hair braided and wrapped into a tight bun like a ballet dancer's. Until then she usually wore it shoulder length and straight.

'I liked it the way ya had it,' he told her.

'But I didn't,' she said. 'It made me look ten years older an too housewifey.'

'If ya didn't want ta look like somebody's wife why'd ya become one?'

'Cut it out, Joe.'

'*You* cut it out. You're becoming a real bitch, ya know that?'

'Maybe my parents were right,' she said, 'that I'd regret the day I married you.'

'A REAL *BITCH!*'

She got up and started to walk into the living room.

He got up and blocked the doorway so she couldn't get by.

'I'll show ya how you'll regret marryin me . . . ' He stood there looking at her but she wouldn't look back.

'I'LL SHOW YA!' He slapped at the air between them. 'C'MON, C'MON, I'LL SHOW YA!' He raised his hand ın a list but she still wouldn't look at him. She kept her head down, tilted away from him, craned in at the neck, crying.

'An A-one bitch,' he hissed, turning sideways, letting her pass.

He's eating from a container of fried rice he got from the Chinese takeout place on Atlantic Avenue when he hears someone calling his name through the kitchen window. He looks out and sees Dougie Lewis standing down in the street.

'Are ya deaf?' he yells up to Joe. 'Or is ya doorbell broken?'

'Neither,' Joe answers. 'I'll be right down.'

During the last month he'd been talking to Dougie about getting him a winter job in Aspen. Dougie called his boss but all the jobs for the season were already filled. He told Joe they usually do their hiring before, but there's always a few that don't show up and some others that can't cut it. They start filling these slots the first week and he'll call Joe as soon as he knows anything.

Dougie's leaving in the morning. Tonight he and Joe are going to a Halloween party being given by a school-teacher Dougie met out in Colorado last winter. She lives in Bayside but spends her Christmas vacations at the ski lodge where he works. He told Joe that last year, right before she left on New Year's Day, she told him that next year she wouldn't even bother to rent a room since she had spent every night in his anyway.

'I thought you were a trick-or-treater,' Joe explains on their way up the stairs. 'They been ringin the bell all goddam night.'

'You're right, I am. Only you ain't got the kind a treat I want.'

'But I got a beer.'

'That'll do fine for now.'

Joe clears off the table, takes two Buds out of the refrigerator and they sit down.

'Ya hear from Rosie?' Dougie asks.

'Last night. We been talkin on the phone.'

'When she comin back?'

He looks at Dougie. 'We ain't discussed it.'

'Don't worry. When she realizes what she's missin, ya know what I mean, she'll be back.'

Joe doesn't answer.

'If it don't happen right away, maybe you'll spend ya winter in the glorious Rocky Mountains. You'll have the time a ya life. Wait'll ya see the chicks gonna be at this swinging swaree tonight.'

Joe goes inside, then comes back in with an ashtray and a pack of Marlboros.

'. . . An besides, after a long cold winter without ya, *she'll* think different.'

'You don't krrow her,' Joe says.

He's begun to accept the fact that Rosie, at least for the time being, is not there. A few weeks ago he might have responded to Dougie the same way but inside he would have pursued all the hopefulness in the things he was saying.

The first few days he didn't tell anyone, not even Joe Flushing Avenue. He seemed himself. A little quieter than usual, a little more deadpan.

He had quietly built a wall of anger around all but the daily mechanical parts of his consciousness. He was numb.

But the wall quickly began to weaken. There were times when suddenly and without warning it would split a seam. It was like somebody opened the door on a soundproof room, and all the notes of some pandemoniac jungle of music that had been compressed inside fought to be the first ones out.

One night, on his way to get a beer, he noticed the empty

space under the chair where Rosie usually kept, side by side, the white tennis shoes she wore to work.

The next thing he knew was that time had passed and while it was passing he had been flinging himself around the kitchen table, crying and gnashing his teeth.

Then he became furious at himself because he had lost control and was standing there, in the cold light of the open refrigerator, sniveling like a baby.

'Fuck her,' he said out loud. 'So she made up her mind an she took her fuckin shoes with her.'

After his anger had sealed the crack, it would turn around until it was aimed at himself. Not because of any one thing he might have done to screw up the marriage. But at some vague, broader mistake, perhaps the entire last five years. Perhaps at what he fundamentally was and felt he could never *not* be.

He did what was expected of him. Got married, went to work, came home, sat with his elbows on the kitchen table. Bought an air conditioner and replaced the filter whenever it got blocked with soot. Nobody likes their job. You're not supposed to. His father hated his. He did it because he was supposed to. You show up in the morning because it's expected of you. Which was his mistake. Which still is his mistake. You don't do what's *expected* of you. You do what you want. Everybody else does but nobody ever told Joe about it. That's why Iris and Roger think he's an asshole. And they're right. If you do what you're supposed to do, you get it all right back up the ass. You're a *testa di minghia*. In fact it runs in the family . . . *testa di minghia*-itis. It's hereditary. Iris and Roger saw it. Rosie's parents recognized the symptoms. Even Rosie has come to realize it. A hundred and fifty years ago Guiseppe Lazaro got tired of packing donkey shit around the roots of other people's olive trees and picking other people's olives and eating polenta and walking around flapping his arms and pissing

into the wind, so he packed up his family and moved to
Messina, the big city, where he washed the bowls the
dockworkers ate their pasta from and then got a promotion
to cooking their pasta and finally became a dockworker
himself and he thought he was something, Guiseppe, when
he went from peasant to worker, but he was a *testa di
minghia* the whole time, and then his grandson, also
Giuseppe, got on a boat and hauled ass to Brooklyn, *Brook-
a-leen*, and never got farther inland than the Navy Yard,
where he worked the docks — *Testa di Minghia the Second* —
and now *his* grandson, *Giuseppe The Engineer*, walks around
other people's basements and talks to himself, the biggest
testa di minghia of them all . . .

Then, after a crash dive into depression, would come an
equally sudden up.

That night he moved the kitchen chair away from the
wall so there would no longer be a space for Rosie's tennis
shoes to *not* be in. It was on that night that he first called
Dougie to ask him to find him a job out in Aspen. Fuck it.
He'd given notice at Water Resources. No more basements. He was young yet. He had a lot of options. Fuck Iris
and Roger. Fuck Rosie. Fuck everybody.

He could rent a houseboat on the San Francisco Bay and
spend his days drinking beer and listening to Otis Redding.
He could do anything. He had a lot more than five options.
He saw a job posted at the office for engineer's assistants at
the water purification plant under the Whitestone Bridge.
With an A.S. in any kind of engineering or equivalent
experience, they'll start you at sixteen thou. Fuck
everybody. He could even go to school. He's got the GI
Bill, Rosie don't. He could get penny loafers and join a
fraternity. Learn to play a guitar! Rah-Rah-Sis-Boom-
Bah! Watch out. Here comes Joe Sis-Boom-Bah. Joe
Goom-Bah. Hey, watch out. It's Joe the Goombah! Fuck
everybody.

Maybe they'd give him the job just on account of his
name and his years of acquired smarts. He imagined the
interview.

'*Tell me young man. What's your name?*'

'*Joe The Engineer.*'

'*That's perfect.*'

'*And your last job?*'

'*Sucking farts outta subway seats.*'

'*Very good, young man. You got the job.*'

Later that night Rosie called to ask him how he was and
he responded real cool. He told her about his work-day,
asked about hers. She had this way of being concerned yet
distant when they talked on the phone. Joe usually hung
up feeling that he had exposed too much. He'd feel that
against his will he had somehow let it slip that he was
having a much harder time of it than she was. At those
moments he was certain that she would only come back to
him if he could behave like he didn't need her. But that
night he stuck to the facts, his day, her day. None of his
urgency slipped out. Did she notice how much the
temperature had dropped and how short the days were
becoming? He outcooled her.

However, last night when he called to tell her he was
going to a Halloween party and she said she was glad, he
got pissed off. When a man goes to party by himself it's
usually for one purpose. That's something she should
know. But he didn't tell her that. Instead, he went into a
spontaneous ad campaign for the party. There were going
to be a thousand people, champagne, a live band, free
cocaine, the works.

When he had finished she was still glad. *Fuck her*, he said
to himself after he hung up, *fuck everybody*.

22

JOE TELLS DOUGIE he sure owns a lot of stuff.

They're on their way out to Bayside and he's looking at the valises and cardboard boxes he's got crammed into the back seat. Sports jackets, shirts and dress pants in plastic dry cleaner's bags are hanging from the hooks over the rear side windows.

'I bring my whole act out there. Clothes, records. My stereo's in the trunk. I gotta have my stereo. I couldn't get through the winter without my Stevie Wonder albums... *Don't you worry bout a thing... Don't you worry bout a thi-ing Mama...*'

For a few blocks he gives Joe a medley of Stevie Wonder's greatest hits.

'Hey, ya got a costume?' he asks Joe.

'No. Ya supposed ta?'

'Ya don't haveta, but I got one anyway. Look.'

He opens his shirt and shoes Joe a black T-shirt with white lettering. It says, *Per favore, non me rompere i coglione.*

Grazie. Underneath is a picture of a hammer.

Joe knows what it means but he lets Dougie translate.

'Please... don't... break... my... balls... Thank you.'

He points to each word as he translates and ends up with two extra words in the Italian version.

'Ya like it? Johnny Lemons is sellin em. Five bucks.'

'Yeah, great.'

Johnny tried to sell him one last week. He also had barbecue aprons with the same message. He told Joe he was asking five bucks, but for Italians he had a special rate: three. He said that three dollars is what he paid for them and held his hands out in front of him, palms out, to emphasize the fact that he was telling the truth.

They're greeted at the door by Dougie's friend, Lauric. She's wearing a black leotard with black tights and a black derby. She's holding a walking stick with a rhinestone knob in one of her blue-fingernailed hands.

She smiles. There's a black birthmark painted on her right cheek.

She gives Dougie a big hug, says hello to Joe and then steps back to let them in. 'You'll Never Know' by Barry White and a cloud of pot smoke come pouring out of the living room.

'Who are ya suppose ta be?' Dougie asks her.

'You don't know?' She waves her blue fingernails. 'Guess.'

'I don't know... Fred Astaire?'

'Nope.'

She makes Joe take a guess but he doesn't know either.

'Liza Minelli, from *Cabaret*.' She tips her derby and bows.

'Oh yeah,' Dougie says.

'Nice,' Joe adds.

She leads them into the living room, then leaves them and begins dancing with an astronaut in a silver space suit with air tanks, a motorcycle helmet and spray-painted ski boots. Because of the weight and bulk of his costume and because he's still subject to the earth's gravitational pull, he's a clumsy, lead-footed dancer who takes up three times more of the floor than anyone else.

They head for a table across the room, laid out with dips, cheese, bread and all kinds of booze. In order to get there they have to squeeze between the astronaut and a belly dancer with veils, finger cymbals, a purple skirt wrapped on a downward slant across her hips and a blue stone in her navel. Next to the table is a plastic trash can filled with ice and cans of beer.

There are about a dozen people dancing and another dozen scattered around the living room eating and drinking. About half of them are wearing costumes. There are more people in another room off to the left, which seems to be the source of the pot cloud that hovers throughout the whole place.

There's a guy in a green beret and army camouflage pants standing next to Joe and Dougie at the table. He has a plastic tommy gun, a water pistol in his belt, false eyelashes, earrings and bright red lipstick.

He smiles at Joe and Dougie, then looks back at the dance floor.

They look at each other and laugh. Dougie asks Joe if he doesn't think this guy is a perfect example of a 4-F.

'Either that or a lieutenant.'

The guy asks Dougie for a cigarette. He gives him one, lights it with his Zippo and asks him if he's supposed to be Corporal Klinger.

'Nope.'

'A 4-F?'

'Uh-uh.'

'Then what?'

'I don't know. When I sat down and thought about what I'd wear this Halloween this concept came to mind. You might say it's a collage. You like it?'

'Oh, very much.' He looks at Joe, then back at the guy, who's begun to realize the playful malice in Dougie's questions.

Dougie decides to investigate the other room.

'I'm gonna mingle. See ya later.'

The 4-F goes over to the other side of the room and sits on a couch next to three women, all wearing Groucho Marx noses and glasses, one of them smoking a real cigar.

During the five days they were upstate Roger kept asking Joe about Vietnam. He kept his cool for a few days, then he got pissed.

The day after they arrived he and Rosie went fishing at a stream down the road from the cabin. Roger told Joe he didn't believe in killing animals unless it was for survival.

Joe very politely told him they would bring him back a trout for dinner.

He barely got his line in the water when a game warden came by and asked Joe for his license. He had no idea you needed one. In fact, he had no idea the guy was a warden. He looked more like a Texas Ranger. He assured Joe he was a warden, that you needed a fishing license, gave him a twenty-five-dollar ticket and a list of places in the area that issued permits, and then wished him and Rosie a good day.

They fought all the way back to the cabin. So much for their fishing trip. The rest of the vacation was a social event.

The next day, while Iris and Rosie were in town, Roger began asking him questions about his year in Vietnam. What it was like, what his job was.

Joe gave him the basics of a field artillery crew but Roger

wanted details.

'Well, it's like this,' he told him. 'You're on duty a certain number of hours an what ya do is wait. Sometimes weeks go by an ya still waitin. Then some asshole in Recon tells some asshole in Field Arty ta throw twenny rounds at a hillside three miles away cause he smelled a Cong's fart comin from the general direction. There ya go.'

'Jesus,' Roger said. 'How do you know what you hit at that range?'

'Ya don't. First ya shoot a Wilson Picket...'

'A what?'

'Wilson Picket, Willie Peter, white phosphorus. It's a marking round ya shoot over the target. If the forward observer likes the way it goes poof, ya pour on the high explosive rounds. Nobody tells ya more cause nobody knows. If there was anybody on the hillside they sure weren't gonna tell ya.'

Then Roger asks the inevitable question.

'Whaddaya mean, did I kill anybody?' was Joe's response. He was tired of being polite.

'I mean that you knew about...'

'I could be so far away ya'd haveta call me long distance an I could erase your fuckin bungalow and five hundred cubic feet of earth along with it in less time than it takes ta ask a dumb fuckin question like that.'

The next day Roger asked Joe to play Frisbee. He told Joe he hadn't meant to upset him. He didn't know he was so sensitive about it.

Joe asked him if he ever played Sicilian Frisbee and Roger said he hadn't.

The next time Joe threw it, at the same moment he snapped it with his wrist and let it go, he slapped his forearm with his other hand, forming the Italian 'up yours' sign.

Roger didn't think it was funny. Joe told him it was only

a joke, he didn't realize he was so sensitive. Roger went inside. Joe spent the rest of the afternoon throwing the Frisbee up and catching it himself.

The remainder of their five-day visit went pretty much the same.

Dougie comes back out for another beer. Joe grabs one too and follows him back into the other room. Laurie, who's doing a soft-shoe around her walking stick, smiles at Dougie when they pass.

In the other, smaller room, six or eight people are sitting on cushions passing around a joint. Someone tied a red scarf around the light fixture, which obscures everyone's face and blurs the edges of all the objects in the room.

The girl Dougie had been talking to disappeared, so he sits down next to a Carmen Miranda, with her plastic fruit on her head, and translates his T-shirt for her.

She laughs and tells him that she understood it because she took Italian in college and even went there once.

'Oh yeah?' Dougie says. 'Then maybe you'd like ta meet my friend Joe. He's a real Italian.'

He introduces Joe, then himself.

'Hi, Brenda,' Joe says, 'nice ta meet ya.'

'They talk for a while, the Dougie realizes he forgot to translate his T-shirt for Laurie and goes back into the living room.

Brenda's a close friend of Laurie's. They teach in the same school.

She asks Joe if he also likes to ski, since that was how Dougie and Laurie, the reasons for their both being there, met.

He tells her he never tried it but might like to someday.

She begins talking about herself. She's twenty-nine, has never been married and likes to travel. She grew up on Long Island but now lives in an apartment just a few blocks from here. Her parents were divorced when she was thirteen, and her father, who owned a business in the garment district and drank too much, died last year. She has a Siamese cat that just gave birth to six kittens.

'Would you like one?' she asks Joe.

'Nah. I couldn't handle a pet right now.'

'Why?' she asks. She turns her head slightly, inquisitively.

He's a bit put off. *Who the fuck knows why?* He stands up and asks her if she'd like another drink. She's very quick to tell him all about herself. He wonders if she expects him to be as open.

He goes into the living room to get another beer for himself and a glass of wine for Brenda. On his way back he makes it a point to look at her from farther away. Until now he hasn't had the chance. Sometimes you can meet somebody and sit within a few feet of them for hours and still never see them. Especially if you're getting high the whole time and the room is dark.

He follows the line her skirt makes across her hips. Along with the plastic fruit, the skirt, a Hawaiian blouse and a pair of high-heeled sandals make up her entire costume. She's actually very sexy but he hadn't noticed up close. She doesn't seem to identify with it. She seems to tone that part of herself down. Even in such a flamboyant costume.

When he sits down she takes off the plastic fruit. She says the pins were pulling at her hair.

Joe tells her he likes her better that way and she asks him why.

'I don't know. I guess it's because I like people ta be the way they are.'

She tells Joe her father always wanted to be something other than he was. When she was very young he wanted to be a writer but he wasn't any good at it. Then he wanted to be a fashion designer but he failed at that too.

Joe's getting a little spooked at how she keeps bringing up her father. But she's also warm and open and he responds to this.

She asks about him and he tells her he's separated. It's the first time he's used the term regarding himself. Separated. Here, out of his life, with all these strangers and a few beers in him, and a woman who's interested in knowing, it's not such a hard thing to say. But at home, sitting at the kitchen table, he hasn't thought of himself in those terms yet.

'How long were you married?' Brenda asks.

'Five years. At the end of next week anyway.'

'Wow.'

'Yeah. An un-anniversary. I'll have ta drink the *un-cola*.'

'And how long have you been separated?'

'Three months.'

He figures telling someone you've only been separated for one month would scare them off. A man who still lives in a house that smells like it did before his wife left it. A man who's only been separated one month might suddenly burst into tears for no reason. If they were to make love he might stop in the middle and whisper his wife's name in her ear.

But slowly they're getting mellower. Joe finds he can be comfortable with Brenda, who's been drinking wine and smoking joints like a champ. He steers the conversation away from Rosie whenever she gets curious.

Dougie walks in, drunk, and sits down. Laurie snubbed him for the astronaut. She told him she only liked him in Colorado. In New York she finds him boring.

'I told her I'm just as good a stick man at sea level. She didn't even like my T-shirt. Whaddaya think she means?'

'I don't know,' Joe says.

'Neither do I.'

He shows Brenda his T-shirt again, and she tells him he already showed her before.

'Maybe Laurie needs ta see it again. She sure didn't get the message. She's really breakin my balls.'

He gets up and wanders back out.

Brenda tells Joe that whatever Laurie may think of Dougie now, she was sure head over heels when she got back last year.

'Things change,' Joe says.

'They sure do.' She looks at him, trying to reinforce all the meanings, vague and clear, of what they just said.

Joe finds it embarrassing.

He tells her he's thinking of working out in Colorado himself this winter. He hasn't decided yet.

'Well,' she says, 'if you're working out there, I'll come out for my Christmas vacation with Laurie.'

She extends her hand to Joe.

'A deal?'

They shake.

'A deal.'

Joe goes inside and gets another round. Dougie's sitting on the couch between two of the Groucho Marxes. He translates his T-shirt for them, then asks why they're all Grouchos.

'Where's Harpo and Chico?'

They just sit there without answering. One on each side, like catatonic lions on the steps of an old hotel.

The crowd is thinning out fast. By the time they finish their drinks Joe and Brenda are the only ones left in the room.

He goes out again. This time to find out if Dougie's ready but he's already gone. Two of the Groucho Marxes are still there. Maybe he left with the third. Maybe he assumed Joe wasn't going home. Maybe he was so drunk he forgot he came with anybody.

He goes back inside and tells Brenda he doesn't have a ride, but if she'd direct him to Hillside Avenue he could take the bus.

'Sure,' she says. 'I'm going that way myself.'

As they walk she tells Joe her apartment building is on the next block. It costs an arm and a leg and it's only a studio. Her father's apartment in Manhattan, which nobody uses, is three times as large.

'Why don't ya move there?' Joe asks.

'Because I teach out here. It's funny. When I was younger and he was there, I'd of given anything to live there. It had paintings and a great view. He even had a fireplace. I loved everything in it. It's funny. Now that he's gone it's just an apartment, too far from my job to live in.'

'Ya think about your father a lot,' Joe says.

'My shrink tells me I still have a whole lot to work out about him. I only saw him one weekend a month. He always wrote me letters, sent gifts. He even took me to Europe when I graduated high school. But inside I never believed he really loved me. That's what my shrink says. And he told me to talk about it if I need to. Not to feel ashamed. Does it bother you?

'Nah. Ya *should* talk about it if ya want.'

Joe's amazed. Not because she's so into her father. And not at how much she's willing to talk about it. But simply at how unlike him she is.

'This is it.' She points to the eight-story apartment building they're standing in front of, one of several along the block.

Then she tells him if he goes straight for another two blocks he'll find his bus stop.

'Can I walk ya to the elevator or somethin?' Joe asks.

'Sure, but I never use it. I live on the first floor.'

It's after 1:00 A.M. and the lobby is empty. Someone has

hung a jack-o'lantern just inside the round porthole window of the elevator. When they pass, Brenda notices and jumps. She puts her hand on her chest and laughs. Then she takes Joe's arm. Just beyond the elevator is the stairwell.

'There's a sign over the door to the stairs that says, *For Emergency Use Only*. Joe points this out to Brenda. It's all he can think of to say.

'Yeah,' she says, 'but nobody obeys those signs. I'd hate to use the elevator for one flight of steps.'

He opens the door and they start up the stairs.

When they get to the landing, she tells him that only the old people and women with baby carriages use the elevator from the second floor.

As she is telling him this he stops her and turns her toward him. He puts his arms around her waist. She presses one hand, lightly, against his chest.

He can't go through the proper ritual. It takes too long. He has to get past all the layers of conversation, the clothing, all the distance. He has to do it now.

And he has to know he *can* do this, that she wants him to. He can't wait.

He leans her against the wall. He has to get there. Her blouse is open, his tongue down her throat. She wraps one leg around his and he crushes against her.

She knows.

She is soft and she tastes like wine.

He has to touch every part of her he couldn't have touched an hour ago when he just met her, two hours ago when he didn't know her. Cut through like an X-ray. Get there. Get there.

She has her hands inside his pants. Her skirt is pushed up over her belly. At his first touch she is soaked. Everything he's ever lost is there. He'll find it all. Get there.

She tries to guide him inside her. He lifts her . . . get

there... pushes... get there...

He keeps trying, keeps pushing, but he loses it. He's already got what he needed.

'Don't worry, don't worry,' she says. 'It's all right.'

He cut through all the layers. He got inside, to the heart, and she wanted him to. You just touch it. Like a spark jumping a gap. You never really know the exact moment it happens.

'Don't worry,' she says. 'It's so soon and you drank so much.'

She doesn't fully understand. It's not because it's so soon or because he's drunk. It's not because she isn't Rosie. Not because she doesn't feel or smell like her. It *already* happened. He didn't want more. He couldn't.

She starts smoothing out her clothes and buttoning up. Joe leans against the wall.

'Maybe we'll try again sometime.'

She straightens her hair. Joe watches her.

'Sure,' he says. Then he turns and holds her by the shoulders. He's not really there anymore but he means it, at least that he would like to. It will be a long time between now and then, but maybe they will.

'Maybe even in a real bed,' she says and laughs.

Joe's looking down at his sneakers.

'A deal?' She extends her hand.

Joe's still looking down at the rough, painted cement floor.

'A deal?' she asks again.

Joe takes her hand. They shake on it.

'A deal.'

23

JOE AND JOE FLUSHING AVENUE stop at a diner on Myrtle Avenue on their way out to Glendale. Joe came in late and didn't have time for breakfast. Joe Flushing Avenue waits in the car while Joe jumps out and comes back with a container of coffee and a buttered roll.

Less than an hour ago he turned over in bed and watched the numerals 8:59 roll upward off the face of the clock like the eyes of a boxer going down after taking a hard right on the jaw, and then replace themselves, this time from the bottom, with the digits 9:00.

At that moment he realized it was a workday. He jumped out of bed, called Joe Flushing Avenue at work and told him to punch him and wait for him downstairs in the garage under the office.

He didn't shower last night and still smelled faintly of Brenda. He reached down and cupped himself, then brought his hand back up to his nose. He wasn't sure anymore if it was Brenda, or his own sweat, or some combination of both their smells. He remembered her breasts, pushing out of her open Hawaiian blouse. They were larger than the breasts of most women he's known, with wide, pointed nipples like the flowers that cap eggplants.

He took her address and phone number but doesn't think he will ever see her again. He doesn't know why. He just couldn't. At the same time, she is good to think of — especially first thing in the morning.

After his head cleared a little and made room, it got crowded again. This time with the events that led up to last night, then with the five years that preceded them. It occurred to him while he was pulling on his socks that he had another workday to look forward to and, on the whole, not a hell of a lot to look back on.

Up until a few years ago sector teams would switch off picking each other up at home. The one who showed up at the office would punch the other one in, giving him an extra hour's sleep. Then they'd switch off the third day in the week, alternating between Tuesday and Thursday in one week and Monday, Wednesday and Friday in the next, which was only fair.

When Water Resources got wise to this they posted a supervisor at the garage exit. Only when one member of a team was on vacation or officially out sick could a car leave with just one man in it. Now, what sometimes happens, especially on Mondays, is that a line of cars develops, backed up from the supervisor's perch, waiting for second members of sector teams to show up.

When they're out in the traffic Joe Flushing Avenue asks how the party was.

'Okay. How'd ya know about it?'

'Dougie came in last night. Around one. An he was with the weirdest chick ya ever seen. She was wearing rubber glasses with a moustache and a big nose an she wouldn't say nothin ta nobody. Not even ta Dougie. She just sat there pourin down Martells as fast as he could buy em.'

'I was wonderin where he went.' '

'An then Johnny plays "It Was a Very Good Year" on the juke an she starts dancin around the pool table, all by herself, whirlin an dippin like somethin outta *Swan Lake*. I tell Dougie, ya got a real nut job there but he tells me he likes her, he's gonna take her out ta Colorado.'

Joe Flushing Avenue cuts off a blue Chevvy to get out from behind a car that's turning, and the driver honks his horn. He gives him the middle finger through the rear-view. Then he gives him another one out the window to make sure he sees it.

'So anyway I ask him, what's ta like... her witty conversation?'

He turns to Joe and laughs.

'I bet he's feelin different about it this morning.'

They're driving past a cemetery on the left. Many of the monuments and tombstones nearest Myrtle Avenue are splattered with egg stains from Halloween vandals. Along the stone wall that surrounds the graveyard are more egg splatters, broken beer bottles and big white powdery splotches from chalk socks. Joe remembers Halloween vandalism. It comes from being too old to go trick-or-treating and too young to get into the bars.

'How'd *you* do?' Joe Flushing Avenue asks. 'Dougie told me you was with some lady dressed up like Chiquita Banana an lookin like ya had the green light.'

'I did all night.'

'Get ya end wet?'

Joe doesn't answer. They're stopped at a light, and he's watching an old woman, sitting at an open window over a bar, shuffling cards.

'Dougie also told me ya asked him if they was hirin out there. That true?'

'I been thinkin about it.'

'Why? Cause Rosie moved out? Think it over. Wait a while. She'll probably come back.'

'It's cause I'm tired a readin meters.' Joe wishes he could shut him off.

'Be careful. Think before ya do somethin like that. Ya'd be outta work in the spring. No benefits. An ya'd lose all ya seniority.'

'Listen. I don't give a flyin fuck for my seniority. In fact, I'm dyin ta lose my seniority. That's right. As fast as I fuckin can.'

'Suddenly ya shit don't stink?'

'An I'm tired a your bullshit. Ya hate the job as much as I do. How come ya always gotta be the public relations man?'

'NOW YOU LISTEN.' Joe Flushing Avenue's got one hand on the wheel. With the other he's pointing at Joe.

'Get ya fat hand outta my face.'

'What's a matter, ya shit don't stink?'

'Pull this fuckin car over. I quit. That's it. Right now.'

Joe Flushing Avenue pulls over to the curb, then pulls his flashlight off his belt.

'Go for that door handle'–he swings the flashlight like a mace–'an I crack ya fuckin head.'

Joe grabs him by the lapels, shakes him. 'Whaddaya want from me... ?'

'That ya shut ya fuckin mouth AN LISTEN FOR ONCE!'

'TA WHAT?'

'Ta *me*.'

Joe lets go and Joe Flushing Avenue falls back against the door.

'Yeah?' Joe says.

'Remember when ya got outta the army an was lookin for a job an ya couldn't find one?'

'Yeah... ?'

'Ya know how ya got this one?'

'Yeah... I applied.'

'An ya know how come ya applied?'

'I don't know. How come?' He looks out the window.

'Cause ya father called Sonny and said, my son can't find a job, ya heard a anything? So Sonny calls me an I tell em ta send ya down.'

'Really?'

'Yeah, really. They wasn't hirin then. They had a waitin list that was maybe a year long, but I recommended ya. That's why I worry about ya callin in sick all the time, an comin in at whatever time ya feel like, an actin all the time like ya shit don't stink.'

'How come ya never told me this before?'

Joe Flushing Avenue pulls back out into traffic.

'Cause I didn't want nothin for it.'

'An whaddaya want now?'

'Nothin.'

Joe flips down the visor, checks the map and tells Joe Flushing Avenue to make a right at the next light.

This is the cork Joe Flushing Avenue's been saving to shove in his mouth if he ever opened it wide enough, got mad enough, became *really unhappy*.

Getting him this goddam job is nothing to be grateful for. Last year he recommended Rosie's cousin Anthony, and now he's reading meters out in East New York. He doesn't want gratitude. He feels like apologizing.

At the same time Joe does feel beholden. Because he knows that in Joe Flushing Avenue's take on things, it was a big favor. You're supposed to feel grateful for a chance to do what's expected of you. Because your father had a job just like it and because he and some other guys just like him decided they'd give you the chance. And if you don't like it you're telling them there's something wrong with the way they live their lives. The way they see it, if you don't take the opportunity they offer you're an asshole. If you take it you have to be grateful.

Either way you're a *testa di minghia*.

When he thinks of it, most things are different in Joe Flushing Avenue's take on them. Sometimes after a conversation about something they did or saw together, Joe feels like they just sat through a movie together, only the movie Joe saw was *Last Tango in Paris*, while Joe Flushing Avenue swears he saw *Guadalcanal Diary*.

They get to their sector and Joe Flushing Avenue parks the car.

Joe tells him that he's also interested in applying for the engineer's assistant jobs out at the water purification plant. He's not sure they'd hire him since he has no experience, but might give it a shot anyway.

'They don't start hirin till May,' Joe says, 'but they gotta post the job six months early for the guys already workin. It's in the contract.'

'They give ya the same benefits?'

'I think so. An the salary's better.'

'Ya'd be happy? Workin out there?'

'Maybe.'

'Then do it.'

They get out of the car, walk the four blocks to the beginning of the sector, split and head up different sides of the block.

On the third block of the sector Joe goes down into a basement and finds the most elaborate model electric train setup he's ever seen. Aside from a four-foot walkway along one wall and the spaces around the oil burner and the steel pillars that support the house, the trains cover the entire floor.

The old man who answers the door comes downstairs via

the inside steps and proudly shows them off to Joe.

He introduces himself. Smitty. He's a retired subway motorman and has spent the last fifteen years putting the set together.

There are three complete trains, each with its own tracks that run a course of mountains, valleys, tunnels and bridges between a city, complete with skyscraper, mailboxes, buses and little plastic traffic cops, and, on the other side, a small town with telephone poles, a lumber mill and a post office.

There's a diesel engine passenger train, a freight train with a huge black steam engine that spouts real smoke, and a tiny HO-scale train that runs on elevated tracks when it passes through the city, running its shadow over the laned, plastic street underneath it like Jamaica Avenue. In the middle of the whole layout is a trolley that shuttles back and forth between the small town and the outskirts of the big city, which Smitty has named Glendale.

After showing Joe the setup he invites him to try it out. Joe manages to run the passenger train without flipping it off the track, while Smitty, with one hand on each transformer, runs everything else. Joe notices a red and blue tattoo of a naked woman in a sailor's hat, posing with her hands behind her head, on Smitty's left forearm.

He tells Joe that aside from a three-year tour of the Far East, as a guest of Uncle Sam, he was a motorman for forty-one years.

He goes upstairs and comes back with two glasses of lemonade. Then he shows Joe how a lumber car, on the freight train, loads real little wooden logs at the lumber mill in the small town and then unloads them at a depot in the big city.

'I knew every inch of track on every subway and elevated line in the New York City transit system,' he tells Joe. 'Forty-one years.'

He goes on and on, telling Joe about the IRT, the old Myrtle Avenue line, the closed-down Eighteenth Street station with its beautiful mosaics that's now a home for bums. He remembers when subway cars had real leather straps and private compartments at the ends of the cars where guys used to sit with their girlfriends on their way home from the movies. He remembers when you really could get arrested for spitting on a subway platform.

When you work door-to-door you occasionally meet somebody like Smitty. People who live alone and have a lot of talking saved up by the time you get there. The readers call them 'Talkers.' Sometimes they can be crazy and sometimes just boring. They usually repeat themselves over and over, and sometimes you get one who's completely obsessed with one thing or another and can be really scary. That's why the best way to handle them is to smile, agree and get the hell out.

There was this guy in South OZ who said he knew Cab Calloway personally. They still write to each other. He misplaced his most recent letter but if Joe would wait he'd take another look. A lady in Woodhaven, who Joe got two years in a row, couldn't stress enough the importance of buying your eggs at Grand Union. Not the A & P, not King Kullen, not even Key Food. They all get their eggs from the same farm in New Jersey, and at this farm cows piss in the same water the chickens drink from. Once in a while is okay, but if you eat them all the time it works on your system like slow-acting poison. She ought to know. Her husband, God rest his soul, was dairy manager for twenty-eight years.

But Joe feels okay about sitting there and listening to Smitty. He seems friendly and sane and not about to go off the deep end.

He asks Joe how long he's been reading meters, and he tells him five years. Then Smitty goes on.

'They didn't have many guys who knew the track like I did. It took a hell of a lot more than five years ta know em. Especially in the late forties when they was putting in all the new lines. The whole thing was a mess a switches and detours. There was guys motorin the Seventh Avenue line that ended up in Queens. I was the best they had.'

'I bet you were.'

'The best,' Smitty says, 'but I didn't do it for those bastards, I did it for me. During one of the first big strikes they tried ta break it an buy out all us more experienced workers. "Ya deserve three times what the others are makin," they told us but we wasn't sellin. If they coulda bought us they coulda bought the whole thing.'

He shows Joe a button on his transformer that makes a hook on the second car of the freight train take a mail sack, actually a tobacco pouch, from a station in the small town.

'I was the best, only I didn't do it for them. Ya never do a good job for the employer. Never.'

He spits.

'Ya do it cause it suits ya ta do it good.'

Joe realizes that he's lost an hour down there and that morning they were late to start off with. He thanks Smitty for the lemonade and for letting him operate his trains.

Smitty follows him outside and shakes his hand before he goes on to the next house.

He rushes through the last block but is still late getting to the car. Joe Flushing Avenue's leaning against it, eating a hero sandwich.

'What took ya?' he asks Joe.

'I was playin engineer.'

He throws Joe a bag with another hero sandwich in it.

'Olive loaf,' he tells him, 'with Swiss cheese.'

'How much?'

'You can buy tomorrow. Whaddaya mean you was playin engineer?'

'There was this old guy with these great model trains.'
'Smitty?'
'Ya know em?'
'I had em three years in a row. I thought that was where ya were but I wasn't sure which block he lived on... '
He smiles.
'... playin engineer. Maybe this afternoon you'll play meter reader.'

24

JOE WAITS UNTIL EIGHT O'CLOCK for Rosie to call and ask about the party but she doesn't, so he calls her. The line's busy. She's probably trying to call him. He waits.

At 8:30 he tries again and Linda answers the phone. He hears the TV in the background. She tells him Rosie had to work late, she just walked in. Then Rosie gets on and tells him that one of the waitresses at Cassandra's quit and another was out with a bladder infection and she had to work a double shift.

'I can take off my shoes,' she says, 'but I'd love to take off my feet. How are you?'

'Fine.'

'How was your party?'

'Not bad.'

'Didja drink up all that free champagne? Was there really a live band?'

'It wasn't as big as I thought it would be. Ya know Dougie. He exaggerates.'

He'd planned to go into what a great time he had. Omitting Brenda while alluding to some really hot goings-on, but now that he's really talking to her he knows he couldn't really pull it off.

'How are you?'

'Fine. I got accepted ta Queens College.'

'Great.'

'And City College too.'

'City College? Ain't that in Manhattan?'

'Yeah.'

'Why go all the way ta Manhattan?'

''Cause I'm thinkin of livin there.'

'Manhattan?'

'Yeah.'

'Why?'

'I'd like to.'

'You'd *like* to?'

'There might be an apartment. In Iris's building.'

'An when's all this supposed ta happen?'

'Next month. I'm not sure yet.'

'*You're* sure.'

She says again that she's not.

'So whaddawe do now,' Joe asks, 'call a lawyer?'

'We don't want a divorce. Let's wait.'

'Whaddaya mean *we* don't wanna divorce?'

'*Joe.*'

'Ya can have the fuckin air conditioner. It gets hot in Manhattan.'

'Joe.'

He doesn't answer.

'It wasn't working. An it wasn't my fault. Don't cut me off. I couldn't stand it.'

'What about me? Ya tell me not ta cut *you* off. Whose idea was this in the first place? Hah, Rosie?'

'It's somethin we have ta do. I can't say it again. You

weren't happy either.'

'You can have everything... Just leave me a chair an the table... an the TV. It don't get Channel five anyway. Ya can buy a new one.'

'I don't want ta talk about it.'

'Whaddaya want ta talk about then?'

'Think about *my* feelings too.'

'I am. That's why I want ya ta have the air conditioner.'

'Cut it out.'

He doesn't answer. Neither of them speak for a while.

'Still there?' Rosie says.

'Yeah.'

'Anyway, one of the reasons I thought of moving is because Frank's such a pain in the ass. He told the kids I was stayin there because I'm sick and Linda's taking care of me. They said I didn't look sick and he made me tell em I had some kind a disease that didn't show on the outside. He says he doesn't want the kids exposed ta what we're goin through. He's a pain in the ass.'

'I coulda told ya that.'

Rosie laughs.

'He even told the kids ta say a prayer so I'd get better.'

'Are ya *gonna* get better?'

'Let's not start again.'

After they hang up he walks over to Mary's, but the door is locked. He looks in the window and sees Johnny Lemons sitting at the bar. Joe knocks on the window and he lets him in.

Johnny's wearing a *Per favore, non me rompere i coglione* barbecue apron. He just washed the floor and it gives off a piney-ammonia smell as it dries. He's sitting in front of a shell glass half filled with bourbon.

'Sonny died,' he tells Joe.

'When?'

'A couple hours ago. Joe Flushing Avenue's with Mary now. They're makin the arrangements.'

He goes behind the bar, pours Joe a glass of bourbon and caps off his own. Then he comes back around and sits.

'Mary said this afternoon he woke up and saw the Lord's Prayer on the wall of his room. He asked Mary did she see it an she told him, yeah Sonny, I see it too.'

'Jesus.' Joe sips his drink and slowly shakes his head.

'An hour later he was gone.'

'Where are they now? Mary an Joe Flushing Avenue?'

'Over at Fitzsimmons Funeral Parlour on Lefferts Boulevard. The wake's gonna be tomorrow night.'

The last time Joe'd been in Mary's when it was closed was during his welcome home party five years ago. It's a run-down, shitty-looking, spooky place when it's so empty and quiet.

He notices, again, the things he noticed when he first started coming here, like the three coasters that level off one side of the pool table, or the window that faces the avenue, half blocked by curtains and two dusty softball trophies, which he never looks out of the rest of the time he's here. He gets a wave of the feelings he felt five years ago, in the same room, in uniform, with Rosie and his parents. *Welcome Home Joe.* He thought the whole thing was a crock of shit, but he knew that was what he was supposed to feel. Inside he was glad to be home, find work, an apartment, get married.

You first get to know a room by the objects it contains. Then, gradually, you get to know it by the people who are usually in it. Your perception of it narrows to its center and you no longer think of it so much as a physical space. More like an area that you feel a certain way in. You go there when you want to feel that way.

Right now, in this moment, it feels to Joe like he fell asleep at his coming home party and just woke up.

He finishes his drink and tells Johnny he'll see him
tomorrow night. He leaves him sitting there, looking into
his bourbon. The place is haunted and he has to get the hell
out of it.

Joe's sitting in front of the TV. He bought a six-pack on
his way home and he's on his fifth. He's watching *The
Waltons.*

Grandma Walton is sick and in the hospital. It's not like
the hospital Sonny died in, which was bright, shadowless,
filled with people and smooth white and green surfaces.
This one is warm. The bedside lamp throws a deep shadow
against the wooden wall. It's familiar, like a big home. All
the nurses know her. Her own grand-daughter, who
married a doctor a few episodes ago, is one of them.
Grandpa Walton spends the nights after visiting hours
sitting in front of the hospital and watching the light in her
room. He spends the mornings up on top of Walton's
Mountain, which is all his and will be his son, John's, when
he dies, and John-Boy's after that.

One morning John-Boy brings a book of poems up the
mountain and reads one to Grandpa. The poem is about
growing old. It says that the leaves on trees are the most
beautiful and the most alive when they're turning from
green to red. Grandpa appreciates this. Then he tells John-
Boy that they'll all be gone someday, but the mountain will
still be here.

John-Boy agrees. Joe gets up and gets another beer.

On his way back he stops in the bathroom. As he pisses,
he looks at the Pink Lady on the old calendar from Mary's.
Sonny's last days had nothing to do with leaves turning
color. How could people go for that? Sonny was in pain
and couldn't stand his own smell. He slept most of the time
from drugs and weakness. He couldn't even lift his arm to
feed himself.

He goes back inside and there's a commercial on the TV. It's for the Broadway musical *Grease*. A dozen people dressed up like it's still the fifties are standing around an old convertible. Some are singing, some are dancing and one of them is just combing his hair. *The Waltons* is over. He won't find out until next week if she dies or not.

He finishes his beer and goes out for more. When he comes back there's a TV movie on called *The Night of the Lepus*. It's about a herd of giant rabbits that terrorizes a small town in Arizona. A commercial comes on and he goes back to the bathroom. He's on his eighth beer, and by this point he visits the bathroom at least once per beer. Each time he pisses he sees the Pink Lady and the old takeout number underneath.

Things feel like they're falling away from him. He's not doing anything other than living his life, but the things around him, one by one, seem to be detaching themselves. Like Sonny, lying in his hospital bed while his life left him, in pieces, cell by cell.

He wishes it was five years from now and he's somewhere else and happy and maybe even with Rosie and he hears a song that brings him back. It would be so easy from all that distance. The whole thing tied in a bundle. *Oh yeah. I remember those days. When this was this and that was that. I wonder how I got through it all.*

It would be so easy. Things would all have changed simply because time had passed and he wanted them to. It would be like shooting fish in a barrel. Like hitting an object the size of a trash can from eleven miles away.

Rosie didn't want to move out but she did. She doesn't want a permanent separation but it doesn't look good from here. He hardly knew Sonny but his death is a great loss. He knows this. He is knowing this. He can't stay at Water Resources. He has no relationship to it. Or to Joe Flushing Avenue either. He never did. They do no more than exist beside each other. He hardly knows him as he hardly knew Sonny.

He must stop being what he is and become something else. He knows this.

He rips the calendar off the wall, brings it into the kitchen and drops it on the table. Rosie was right. It's a dumb fucking thing to have on your bathroom wall.

He gets another beer.

When he gets back to the TV the giant rabbits are jumping all around a farmyard, knocking over fences, a barn and a silo. One of them overturns a car with its nose.

Anyone could see that they're just little rabbits. They look more frightened than dangerous. The houses and fences and cars look less real than the ones in Smitty's train set.

He gets another beer. When he comes back he changes the channels.

Click... the news... click... more news... click... two men see a white tornado coming out of some woman's kitchen window... click... more news... click... Oscar Madison sprays room deodorizer into Felix Unger's soup... click... snow and static... click... the rabbits again. They're chasing a family who are running toward a church. Just before they get to the steps, the little girl falls. 'Go on!' the father yells to his wife and goes back for his daughter. They make it inside just in time.

If they could combine this movie with *The Attack of the Fifty-Foot Woman*, they could have her take a pregnancy test. Joe goes back to the kitchen for another beer.

When he comes back he's got the calendar with him. He drops it on the couch. He's sitting next to the Pink Lady.

He picks it up again, goes to the phone and dials the number.

A woman answers.

'Hello?'

'Hi.'

Silence.

'Hello?'

'Didja know this number useta ring in the kitchen of a restaurant an the cook who worked there useta make Mayor Wagner's lunch?'

'What?'

'Yup. It's true.'

'Is this some kinda joke?'

'Nope. I'm serious.'

'Ronald. Is that you? Always jokin.'

She laughs.

'No, it's not. It's Joe The Engineer an the cook I was tellin ya about is named Sonny, only it was really Joseph too.'

'Yeah sure. Joe the what? Ronald, you're hysterical. Wanna talk ta ya brother? He just got in. Ya know, Wednesday, bowlin night.'

'No. Believe me. I'm serious. His name was Sonny an he died today. I was just watchin this movie where a bunch a rabbits were going around killin people... '

'You saw that too... ?'

'... an I'm the only one here. Everyone else's gone an I guess I been drinkin too much... '

'This isn't Ronald.'

'My name's Joe. I told ya.'

'Who is this?' A man's voice. Louder and threatening. 'Who's *this*?'

'You called. You tell me.'

'Ronald.'

'This ain't Ronald.'

'You're right. It's the Pink Lady. Ronald's dead.'

'A pervert, hah? Listen, asshole. If ya had any balls ya'd tell me who ya really was an then I'd come over there an bust ya fuckin head.'

'Now *you* listen, motherfucker. I *am* a pervert. A dangerous one. Worse than Son a Sam. Ya never heard a the Pink Lady? Ya never will. Cause right now I got a howitzer One-O-Five aimed right at your house an during the next commercial I'm gonna blow you, your wife an your fuckin bowlin ball inta fertilizer.'

Click.

'Got it? Hey, motherfucker. Got it?'

He tells the dial tone to go fuck itself and slams down the receiver.

He falls back on the couch and the room begins to spin. The perky theme song from *Joe Franklin's Memory Lane* makes it spin faster. He leans over, turns down the sound but leaves the set on. Joe Franklin, Joe Flushing Avenue, Joe/Sonny, Joe The Engineer . . . *A good night to you all and to all a good night.*

25

AT 8:30 Joe Flushing Avenue calls. Joe, still asleep, gets up and answers the phone. He will not remember the call. Joe Flushing Avenue tells him he's going to call in, take the day as personal time since the wake starts at 1:00. If Joe wants he'll call in for him too. It would be better that way. They're getting tired of hearing his voice this time of the morning.

Joe gets up, goes into the bathroom and comes back into the living room. When he gets back to the couch he begins to wake up. For the first time he notices that the TV is still on from the night before with the sound turned all the way down. There's a news reporter talking on the screen. Just over his silent talking head is another screen on which a film is showing. Two young black men in handcuffs are being led into a police station. One of them tries to hide his face from the cameras. The other one doesn't seem to care. Then their images fade from the screen and are replaced by the words: *Next: Is your kitchen really a danger zone?*

*　*　*

Just after 9:00 the phone rings and Joe wakes up again. It's Dougie, long distance, from Colorado.

He tells Joe that the lodge didn't expect enough early snowfall so they're hiring extra slope workers just in case.

'I told em I knew somebody that could do it. All ya do is follow the spreader and make sure it's all flat. It's hard work but ya don't work that much. Ya just gotta be on call. Just waitin. Ya get room and board, an Easter ya go home with three grand. By the end a the season ya might be drivin a spreader. Spreaders get four grand. Whaddaya say?'

'I don't know, I just woke up.'

'Look, Joe, take my number. They gotta know by Monday, so decide quick and call me... By the way, how'd ya make out with Chiquita Banana?'

'Brenda?'

'Yeah, whatever, she had *some* fruit.'

When Joe hangs up he goes to the bathroom again. When he gets back to the couch he backtracks slowly up the series of events that foggily become the night before. Before, he didn't wake up enough to realize that his hangover could sink a ship.

He picks up the phone and calls in to the office, and Nettie tells him that Joe Flushing Avenue already called in for him. He thanks her and hangs up.

On the TV screen is the face of a middle-aged man wearing a beret. Across the screen over his head are the words *FOUR MILLION*. Joe leans off the couch and turns up the sound.

'In exchange for a ransom of four million dollars, Dutch multimillionaire Maurits Caransa was released by kidnappers who abducted him last Friday in front of his home in Amsterdam.

'Mr. Caransa, who was unharmed, said he had been treated well but had no idea where he was at any time because he was always blindfolded and kept constantly moving. He was never in the same place for more than half a day.

'Police said that common criminals, not terrorists, were responsible for the kidnapping of the sixty-one-year-old real estate man.'

Joe turns off the TV and falls back onto the couch. From under the small of his back he pulls out a ball of wrinkled paper which is all that's left of the Pink Lady.

He lies with his cheek against the slightly rough surface of one of the wheat-colored flower designs embroidered in the upholstery of the couch. From up close he can see that it's not a flat regular pattern at all, but a clump of tan threads, rising through the interstices of a lighter tan fabric, arcing like the curl in Fabian's D.A. and going back inside. Upon further inspection it seems even more imperfect, with all the threads coming from different parts of the lighter grid of thread and diving back into others. After a while, with his nose so close it's touching the center of the flower, it looks like a clump of dried grass that somebody stepped on.

At 11:00 Rosie calls from work.

'Listen, I heard about Sonny. I called you at work an they told me you took the day off. Goin ta the wake?'

'Yeah.'

'I'd like ta go together.'

'Okay.'

'Is it?'

'Ya still movin?'

'I haven't decided.'

'*You've* decided.'

'I haven't. Let's not go into it . . . a truce . . . okay?'

'Yeah.'

'Is your suit ironed?'

'Was it ironed the last time ya hung it up?'

'When was that?'

'Ya cousin Anthony's wedding. Last year.'

'I think so... '

'Then it's ironed.'

'Ya better check anyway.'

'I'm thinkin a takin a job in Colorado. Where Dougie works.'

'Doin what?'

'Makin snow.'

'Are you kiddin?'

'Nope. He just called up. Long distance.'

'When did all this come about?'

'I been thinkin about it for a while now.'

'What about that water purification job you were talkin about?'

'This sounds like more fun.'

'Are you *that* unhappy?'

'I'm fine.'

'Then why would you go all the way to Colorado?'

'Why'd you go ta Manhattan?'

'That's different.'

'Why?'

'I thought we had a truce.'

'Yeah, a truce.'

'Please, Joe.'

'Okay... By the way, there's one possible new career in my future. I'm thinkin a becomin a kidnapper. I saw this guy on the news this morning... '

'That Dutch guy?'

'Yeah.'

'Do you believe it? I was just readin it, in the *Post*.'

'Think they'll get caught?'

'Not if they're smart. Ya can't touch nobody who's got four million.'

'What would you do with four million?'

'I don't know, but when I figured it out I could afford to do it.'

Joe exhausts the muscles he's been using to keep the conversation in neutral and asks Rosie how Iris and Roger are.

'They broke up.'

'I guess we've started a trend. How'd it happen? I thought they had so much in common.'

'What does that mean?'

'Just what I said. Anyway, now they're free ta make two more people miserable.'

'You are *unhappy*.'

'About them? I'm heartbroken. What's poor Iris gonna do?'

'Let's get off it.'

'Let's *stay* off it.'

'Look. I gotta set up, it's way past eleven. I gotta work a double shift again, so I'll change at Linda's and come by at six-thirty. Make sure the suit is pressed. I think my black shoes are in the closet. Christ, Lorraine's pointing at the clock. It's eleven-thirty. I gotta go.'

26

IF YOU COULD lift up the entire structure of the Fitzsimmons Funeral Home and then set it down, right in the middle of a wealthy suburban community, no one would realize it was a funeral parlor. It would appear to be just another sprawling suburban house, being where it belongs, among the similar homes of successful lawyers, businessmen, urologists.

In Richmond Hill, however, even if it lacked the black-top parking lot and its large and discreet sign, a little girl who might, while driving past with her father, tap him and ask, 'What's that big building, Daddy?' would invariably be told, 'That one, honey? That one's a funeral parlor.'

Split-level, three floors high, it takes up four or five of the tract-house-sized lots that cover the rest of the block. The stones set irregularly in its tan mortar walls run a subdued spectrum from beige to brown. The outside of the structure shows no painted wood, no brick, no shingles. In Richmond Hill it would have to be a funeral home. If it weren't maintained as well and had pieces of construction paper with crayon drawings by children scotch-taped to the windows, it might pass for a library. If it had brighter lights and let out the sounds of live music, it could be a catering hall.

In the entryway, just inside the two sets of glass doors is the office, with its coffered blond-oak door and the directory, white letters on black plastic, arranged like a table of contents with room numbers instead of pages. Tonight there are eight wakes in progress. When the demand requires they can house up to twelve.

Just beyond that point a hall intersects the entryway. To the left are four wake rooms or chapels, three of which are in use. To the right is the elevator and the lounge. Against the wall, a few feet from the elevator, is a bronze head of Hermes. You know it is Hermes because his name is chiseled into the black marble pedestal. The staffs on all the letters are cut too long or on odd angles to give the impression of being Greek letters.

Hermes, besides being messenger of the gods and patron of businessmen and thieves, had the job of guiding the dead to the underworld. The underworld, in those days, was not hell but where everybody went.

Rosie is explaining this to Joe, leaning against the wall next to the sculpture.

'Except for people who were really great. Then they made you into a god and you were immortal.'

'I remember that from high school. An there was that guy who was king a the underworld,' Joe says.

'Pluto?'

'No, Frank Nitti.'

'Gimme a break.'

Sonny's eight-year-old nephew, Michael, is playing elevator operator, taking people up to the second and third floors where there are more wakes going on, or down to the restrooms and pay phones in the basement. Every time he stops at the first floor he asks Joe and Rosie if he can take them anywhere.

'How about Hawaii?' Joe asks.

'Can't go anywhere outside the building.'

'Oh,' Rosie says, as if she hadn't realized that until just then.

Sonny is laid out in the first room off the entryway. They had already been inside, where twenty or twenty-five of Sonny's relatives and friends are sitting in the rows of aluminum folding chairs facing the open coffin. To the right are four deep-cushioned chairs. Mary and Sonny's mother sit in two of them. After kneeling in front of the casket, people stop and sit next to them, lean close and talk for a moment.

Sonny's two brothers and their wives are there. Johnny Lemons is sitting on a couch in the back of the room with one of Sonny's cousins. When Joe and Rosie stopped by to say hello, he was in the process of guessing the name brands of the guy's suit and shirt without seeing the labels.

'What's your neck size?' he asked him, examining his collar with a look of serious, professional acuity. 'Fifteen, right?' He rolled his gum over to the other side of his mouth. 'I can tell just by lookin.'

Joe Flushing Avenue was standing by the door. He looked unhappy and unsettled, like an animal being petted the wrong way against its fur. His eyes showed he was still coming off a bad night. He'd spent the afternoon and most of the evening walking around the room, trying to attach himself to one conversation after another but had no luck. Finally he planted himself by the door, next to Ainooch, an old friend of Sonny's father from Navy Street, who's at least eighty and has a vegetable stand out in Flatbush that he still manages to open every morning.

'What else I gotta do?' he told Joe and Rosie. 'My wife, she's gone three years. What else I gotta do?'

He opened the stand over forty years ago. He tells them the whole story. Now people come from all over the city to buy from Ainooch.

'Ya know why?... All these years I always get the best an never cheat nobody. They ain't just customers, they're friends. I get the best. You come by sometime, you see... You come by.'

'We'd love to,' Rosie told him.

Now, standing out in the hall, Joe tells Rosie he wishes she wouldn't refer to *us* as *we*, in terms of doing anything.

'I was just being polite. He was talkin ta both of us. Besides, I don't think he really expects us to go there.'

'That ain't the point.'

'What *is* the point?'

The elevator door opens and Michael waves to Joe and Rosie. It closes. A thin ray of light descends between the doors.

'Ya can't all of a sudden start actin like we're together just cause it's easier.'

'What am I supposed to say? We'd love ta come but we're separated at the moment. Tell ya what. I'll come Wednesday, Joe the following Saturday...'

'CAN IT, ROSIE!'

'Lower your voice... All right, all right, I'm sorry.'

A minute passes and neither of them says anything. An attendant, carrying a wreath attached to a green aluminum tripod, comes in through the glass doors and walks down the hall.

'I guess it don't really matter what ya say. It's if ya really want to, I mean, do stuff like that.'

'Like what?'

'Go out ta this guy's vegetable stand. With me, I mean.'

Rosie looks at him. 'You were just mad cause I said *we*. Now ya want us ta go together?'

'I don't know. Maybe we should do stuff together.'

'Look, Joe. I said it cause I can't think of anything else in the future. I'm not useta thinkin another way yet.'

'That's cause ya don't want to... Listen, Rosie...' He turns so he is closer and facing her, his hand against the wall over her head. 'Move back home. I know it was hard. For me too. But bein apart ain't gonna help. It's been over a month now.'

'I can't.'

'Why, Rosie, *why*, dammit?'

'During the last few years you *didn't* want ta do anything with me. Now ya want ta go out ta this guy's vegetable stand? Now ya want ta...'

'Don't lay that shit on me, Rosie. Not now. We both fucked up. I don't know what it means but I know what we feel.'

'I don't know anymore. What *do* we feel? Just that we're beginning ta know what it's like apart. If it's better. I'm just beginning ta feel what it's like.'

'Ya want ta know what it *feels* like...' He turns away, then turns back again like he's going to say something, but instead shoves the head of Hermes and it tilts on its pedestal and bangs the wall. It rocks back to a standstill, making a hell of a lot of noise.

Everyone turns. Mr. James L. Fitzsimmons pops his head out of the office door, looks over his half-glasses to make sure everything is all right, then closes the door, gently, clicking it shut with a solid, slow, two-part click that befits the office of funeral director and sets an example of proper solemn behavior for whoever it was that had made all the noise.

Rosie's looking down. There are tears in her eyes. Joe is also looking down with his arms crossed. A woman in an old-fashioned hat with black lace over her eyes leaves a chapel farther down the hall. On the way out she passes Joe and Rosie and thinks to herself that these two young people must have lost someone very close.

Mr. Fitzsimmons leaves his office and presses the elevator button. When it arrives Rosie tells Joe that she has to go down to the ladies' room. At this point he realizes she's crying, but she breaks away and slips into the elevator as the doors are closing.

Joe goes back into the chapel and walks up to Sonny's coffin.

He's pissed at himself for even bringing it up. She's not moving back home. If she were it would have to be her move. And the more he needed her, the less likely she'd be to make it. She's not coming back anyway. Fuck it.

Whoever combed Sonny's hair didn't part it where he used to, but nearer the center, in a younger, post-sixties style that causes the remaining front hairs to sweep to the sides and cover more of the skin usually exposed by his receded hairline. He's wearing a dark blue suit and blue tie. In his lapel is a little gold cross from the Holy Name Society of St. Michael's in Red Hook, where he was baptized. All of his exposed skin, even the hands, folded over his deflated abdomen with rosary beads entwined in the fingers, are covered with flesh-toned makeup.

No matter how hard Mr. Fitzsimmons and company have tried, they failed to make Sonny appear as if he were simply asleep.

Next to the coffin are several wreaths, pots of flowers and a table spread with Mass cards. In the center of a large wreath of red and yellow roses is a cardboard clock with hands set at 3:30, the hour at which Sonny passed on. There's a card attached to a red ribbon at the base, with the names of Sonny's brothers and their wives.

Joe goes back to the door, where Joe Flushing Avenue

and Ainooch are still standing. He leans against a little oak shelf with a book for visitors to sign as they leave. Next to the book is a stack of funeral cards.

On the front of each one is the image of Jesus Christ and the message: *Come to Me, All You Who Labor and Are Burdened, and I Will Give You Rest.*

On the back are two short prayers and these words:

Of Your Charity Pray For The Repose
Of The Soul Of
Joseph Anthony Catanzaro
November 2, 1977

J. L. Fitzsimmons, Funeral Director

There are people as old as Ainooch, standing there, drifting back and forth over his cane, who have hundreds of these cards in their dresser drawers, against the time when they might need them, to remember.

'Why don't ya sit down?' Joe asks him.

'I like ta stand. Better for the circalation.'

Joe nods.

Rosie walks back into the room, passes between them and goes over to one of the empty seats next to Mary.

Ainooch tells Joe about how he and Sonny's father had been friends. Then about his own childhood in Italy.

'My father, he was a carpenter, a *carpentiere, ha gabeet?*' Yeah.'

'An I was his apprentice. He died when I was fourteen an my mother comes here ta live with her sister. Otherwise I still be in Messina.'

The elevator door opens out in the hall and Joe hears Michael's eight-year-old voice saying, 'Going up? Anybody going up?'

'Anyway,' Ainooch goes on, 'the apprentice had ta be at all the funerals cause it was his job to nail the coffin shut.'

Joe Flushing Avenue leans closer. He knows the story by heart but has nothing else to do with himself. He watches Joe listen, smiling, as if he were telling it himself.

'Whenever it came time the women would go crazy, screamin and sometimes hittin an scratchin me too, like it was my fault. Once this lady jumps on my back and starts yellin, *Demonio! Demonio!* While her mother-in-law grabs my hammer, takes a swing and catches me right on the nose.'

He turns sideways to show Joe how crooked his nose is. 'Ya see, if I'm walkin down a street an there's a dog shittin in both gutters, I can tell the one on the left first... ' He laughs and pretends he's walking, then smelling something bad to his left, then his right. 'Understan?'

'Yeah,' Joe answers.

'Anyway my nose is bleedin like mad so I walk away, right off the job. That night my father beats the shit outta me. *Maron.* In those days it was hard ta find work. But I tell em I didn't give a shit an ya know what he does?'

Joe Flushing Avenue smiles.

'He hits me right in the nose. Ya see, it wasn't the old lady that broke it, it was my father.'

He turns his head again to show the crooked profile of his nose.

Until now they hadn't noticed Mr. Fitzsimmons standing behind them. He asks them if the boy on the elevator belongs to anybody in the room. He stands there with his hands clasped, addressing all three of them.

'Yeah,' Joe answers. 'Why?'

'Someone will have to get him off. *I* asked him. He won't leave.'

'Why?'

He unclasps his hands. 'The elevator is for the use of the people who come here. It's not a toy.'

'But he lets everybody ride. He just wants ta push the

buttons.'

'He'll have to get off.' His voice has reached a firm, annoying pitch, like Mr. Whipple asking three housewives to please stop squeezing the Charmin.

'Ah, leave him alone,' Joe Flushing Avenue says. 'What does a kid know from wakes.'

'Get him off!' Mr. Fitzsimmons has raised his voice. Something a good funeral director never does. As if by magic, a tall attendant appears in the hall right behind him.

It's the sudden appearance of this goon, obviously here to threaten or protect somebody, that puts the idea in Joe Flushing Avenue's head that he's about to do something violent.

He swings back his arm and lands a right on Mr. Fitzsimmons's jaw. It's a bad connection, high, more finger than knuckle, but enough to send him staggering back out into the hall.

Joe is shocked. Ainooch is shocked. The goon follows them out of the chapel, as stunned as his boss, unable to respond without orders.

At this moment a loud wail comes from inside the room. There are times, at wakes, when mourners, empty for a short time of their sadness, are given a moment's rest. Then there are moments when the enormous weight of their loss suddenly descends on them like a safe dropped from a window. For Mary this is one of them.

Rosie and Mary's sister-in-law are trying to hold her back as she tears at the lapels of Sonny's jacket.

Joe looks in for a moment and sees that there are tears in Rosie's eyes too.

Joe Flushing Avenue just stands there for a second, listening to Mary's fit of crying. Then he hits Mr. Fitzsimmons two more times. The second one knocks him against the elevator doors. As he slides down, unconscious, they open and he falls between.

Michael looks out at Joe Flushing Avenue and at the attendant. Then down at the man who had yelled at him before, lying half in, half out, of the elevator.

The attendant swings Joe Flushing Avenue around and hits him once in the mouth. He goes down, right where he stands, like somebody just filleted his legs.

Ainooch, getting mad, bangs his cane against the floor.

Next the goon heads for Joe, but he meets him on the way over, throwing a deep punch into his stomach. The goon doubles over. Then backs out the glass doors with his arms wrapped around his middle.

Joe Flushing Avenue is lying in the middle of the floor, unconscious. Michael keeps pressing buttons, but each time the elevator doors try to close they bang against Mr. Fitzsimmons and open again.

Mary lets out one more long moan, in anger at who- or whatever had let her husband live as he had during the last years. Then, calmer, she puts her hands over Sonny's shrunken fingers and tells him not to worry, she'll be with him soon.

When the goon comes back in he's got three parking-lot attendants in tow. The Hoover Dam in Joe's head that stood between him and his anger explodes, or rather, disappears, leaving no debris, no remnants of control.

He kicks the glass door before they even get through it. Then he gets the big one as he comes in with another deep sidewinder to the stomach. He just stands there, doubled over, so Joe takes a wild swing at the guy standing behind him but misses.

Ainooch is frightened, seeing so much anger come out of Joe, who takes another swing at the guy behind the doubled-over goon and misses again. This time he swings back and catches Joe in the jaw but he doesn't feel it, he only hears it.

By this time Johnny Lemons gets wind of the fight, and he, along with Sonny's brothers and some of the other guys, pile out the half of the doorway not blocked by Ainooch.

Another attendant walks in carrying a wreath that has just been delivered. Joe grabs it, swings it against the head of the guy who just hit him and loses it, like a baseball player losing the bat. It bounces off the wall behind him and lands on top of Joe Flushing Avenue. Rest in peace.

Sonny's brothers are swinging it out with the two other attendants, pounding their anger at the loss of their brother into these two men, who have no idea who started this fight or why they're fighting it.

Mary and Sonny's mother remain in their chairs at the front of the room while everybody else either squeezes out the door or stands just inside it, watching.

Michael manages to shove Mr. Fitzsimmons out from between the doors and goes off to another floor, where there are only people who are dead or people who are being sadly quiet.

When the goon straightens up he catches Joe in the chin with his head. Joe staggers back a step, giving the guy an opening for a hard right which he takes right on the nose and upper lip. Joe takes a wild, low swing and catches him in the solar plexus. He stumbles backward out into the hall between the two sets of doors. This time he stays there.

Joe turns his head and Rosie shrieks when she sees the blood pouring from his nostrils and upper lip.

He kicks the thick glass doors over and over again. They rattle and gong but are too thick to break. He turns around and takes a swing into a haze of moving bodies but no one's near enough to reach, so he turns again and this time kicks the oak door to Fitzsimmons's office until the latch breaks and it swings open.

Just before the police arrive, Johnny Lemons manages to wrench Hermes' head off its pedestal and hurl it, in a slow, heavy air, at one of the attendants. It drifts over the head of one of Sonny's brothers like time-lapse footage of a sunset and hits the floor with a loud, echoing thud. Being solid bronze, the head remains intact but henceforth its nose will be as crooked as Ainooch's.

The cops think the noise is a gunshot and run in with pistols drawn. Johnny Lemons raises his hands, turns toward the wall and spreads. All the others, except Joe, stop where they stand. He's still swinging wildly but not hitting anyone.

'JOE, STOP, PLEASE, it's over!' Rosie yells.

'STOP IT JOE!' one of the cops shouts, having learned in the police academy that someone's name has a more controlling effect than *Mack, Buddy,* or *You.* Joe doesn't stop because he only half hears them and, besides, there are at least two other Joes around, one lying on the floor, the other inside in a coffin.

Finally the cop throws him against the wall, pressing his nightstick against his chest to hold him still. Joe looks straight at him for a second. Then gives him a great big smile.

Rosie comes over and puts her arm under Joe to hold him up, and the cop leaves off.

No one will give them a straight answer as to exactly what happened or who started it. What they *do* know is that there are two men lying unconscious on the floor. They call an ambulance and take down everyone's name and address in case they decide to book anyone later.

Rosie is standing there, holding Joe with her knee against his knee and her shoulder against his chest. He's leaning his head down, against hers, still smiling.

The elevator doors open and Michael steps off for the first time all night. When he sees the policemen taking everybody's names, he wants them to take his too, but they tell him they don't want to.

Joe Flushing Avenue and Mr. Fitzsimmons leave for the hospital in the same ambulance. They take the tall attendant along too.

Finally Michael makes such a pain in the ass out of himself that one of the cops agrees to take his name.

'We don't need your last name,' he says, looking at the boy, 'Michael is enough.'

27

ROSIE WRAPS some ice cubes in a washcloth, brings it into the bedroom and lays it gently across the bridge of Joe's nose. The left side is so swollen that it's as wide just below his eyes as it is at the nostrils. She tells him to hold still and just lie there. Then she goes into the bathroom, soaks another washcloth, wrings it out, comes back into the bedroom and begins washing the dried blood from his nostrils, upper lip and chin.

She flinches when she touches the bruised skin, but he tells her it doesn't hurt a bit. She tells him he looks like Lincoln on a penny that just got rolled over by a subway train, and he tells her not to be so funny. She rinses out the washcloth and comes back. Then she tells him that she wasn't trying to be funny, but it looks like it should hurt and in the morning it probably will.

His upper lip has also begun to swell and his entire nose, as well as the skin around it, is a dark burgundy red that, in a few hours, will condense into a tender black-and-blue.

She tells him it might hurt less if he doesn't look into a mirror for at least a week, and he tells her she's being funny again.

'Just lie still for a while,' she tells him. Then she goes into the living room, picks up the ashtrays and empty beer cans and brings them into the kitchen.

After the cops went away everyone put on their coats and slowly left as the attendants picked up Hermes' head, cleaned and vacuumed the hallway and locked up the Catanzaro chapel room for the night.

Rosie shouts from the kitchen that Joe is a goddam slob. He thanks her for the compliment, then asks her to call the hospital again. She had called earlier, when they got home, but there was no news for them.

This time they tell her that Joe Flushing Avenue and James Fitzsimmons both had minor concussions — no fractures or brain damage — and have been released. The tall attendant, whose name, the nurse tells Rosie, is Francis Davie, is being held overnight for further tests.

She comes back into the bedroom, sits next to Joe on the bed and tells him what the hospital told her.

'They can't have too good an X-ray machine though,' she adds.

'Whaddaya mean?' Joe says from under his washcloth.

'They X-rayed Joe Flushing Avenue's head and didn't find any brain damage.'

'I come home with Rosie Lazaro an now I got Jack Benny.'

She looks down at him. He turns her, slightly, and slips his hands under her blouse.

At first she responds like his hands are cold even though they're not. Then she just sits, watching him, watching the backs of his hands move in slow circles inside her blouse.

What he needs at the moment pays no attention to the condition the rest of him is in.

'It's gonna kill ya in the morning,' Rosie says.

His eyes follow the pressed seam up the sleeve of her white cotton blouse. It rises, falls, winds its way up her arm like the Great Wall of China. It reminds him of a photograph he once saw of it in a structural engineering text. He tells her this and she laughs.

'It's gonna kill ya in the morning,' she says again.

They make love, half undressed, slowly. For a moment they reassemble the feelings that had broken apart, bit by bit, and had settled in the daily elements of their life together, taking on their dull, inert identities: refrigerator, chair, soap dish, pot holder, air conditioner, light switch. For a moment they reclaim it, leaving these objects cold, depersonified, simply what they are.

Afterwards they undress each other and lie on top of the blankets. Joe slides down and lays his head on her belly. He wets his fingertips and lightly rubs her nipples, making them hard, softer, hard again.

They just lie there for a while, not speaking.

Time passes and they begin to get cold, so they slip under the blankets. Rosie leans off the bed, turns the lamp off and settles with her head against Joe's shoulder.

'You're my wife,' he says.

She hears him, but she doesn't answer.

'You're my wife,' he says again, not to make sure she heard it but to reaffirm it, to make it a more certain fact.

She still doesn't answer. She reaches over and holds his cheek in her hand.

'Rosie?' He lifts his head, drops it back again.

'Yeah?'

'I said you're my wife.'

'I know.'

'Well, are ya?'

'Yeah... but we're not married, not now anyway.'

'We ain't divorced.'

'An we're not married either.'

'Whaddaya mean?'

'I don't know.'

'But ya love me. Ya do.'

'Yeah, I do, you love me, so what? Lotsa times you didn't. Lotsa times I didn't . . . '

Joe lifts his head.

'It's like . . . '

'What?'

'It's like lovin somebody has nothin ta do with bein in a relationship with em.'

He could say bullshit. Not understand. But he can't — he does. There's been enough banging his head against the wall. Enough fighting things as they really are.

As they really are.

Two people who've lived together five years and who now, two months after the fact, find themselves in the sack again . . . who've bathed together like brother and sister, who have, on a few occasions, slipped into each other's lives and bodies like there had never been any defenses or armor around people in the entire history of human beings . . . and who've, at times, felt the act of sharing the same table, or bed, or room even, seemed an unbearable intrusion . . . who've spent long and longer periods without ever climbing out of their separate inertias to exchange a word, a gesture with any meaning or feeling . . .

Simply what it is.

What is it?

A *testa di minghia* would call it a marriage.

Rosie asks if his bruises have started to hurt. His face is warm against her hair. With his sleepy mind he reaches out to the bruised areas, tries to bring back some sensation, but still feels nothing.

'You got aspirin?' she asks.

A month is enough time for the first series of

replacements aspirin, soap, toilet paper-to happen. Were she living there, she would know.

'I think so.'

'Good,' she says. 'It'll hurt in the morning.'

'Ya keep sayin that. How do ya know for sure?'

'Cause it's killin me already.'

28

IT'S 11:30 MONDAY MORNING. Joe's walking toward the car to meet Joe Flushing Avenue for lunch. His nose is swollen like a boxer's and his upper lip is twice its usual size. On Saturday morning he woke with the throbbing headache Rosie had predicted. Today is the first day he can talk without it hurting.

They spent the morning cleaning up the *not homes* and *no accesses*. Joe visited twenty-one addresses. Of the eleven *not homes*, one is now home and read. The ten *no accesses* still offer no access.

From a distance he sees what, at first, appears to be a white flag hanging from the car's antenna, but turns out to be an enormous pair of men's boxer shorts. He knows how it got there. When someone gives Joe Flushing Avenue a hard time he gets even by stealing something from their basement: a screwdriver, a can of tuna fish, a bra, a bottle of wine. Something they may never even notice is missing.

This morning Joe Flushing Avenue has other reasons to

be upset. On their way out to Glendale Joe told him he had
given notice this morning and was leaving for Colorado a
week from Wednesday. He called Dougie on Saturday
morning. Next Wednesday, November 15, is the last day
he can show up and still find a job waiting. Joe also told
him he can make it back in time to take the engineer's
assistant exam this spring if he wants to.

Joe Flushing Avenue is leaning against the front fender,
his hands in his pockets, watching Joe approach. There's a
large swatch of white gauze surgically taped to the right
side of his forehead with black-and-blue skin showing at
the edges. His right eye is bloodshot.

He tells Joe that some bitch told him to take his shoes off
before going into her basement. He told her he'd do it if she
took her dress off. A moment later he was writing the words
no access on her sector card.

It was her next-door neighbor who paid for her sins as
well as his anger at Joe's quitting. A lonely, overweight
bachelor, who politely welcomed Joe Flushing Avenue,
personally guided him to the water meter and then
trustfully went back up the stairs.

Both Joe Flushing Avenue and James L. Fitzsimmons
came to on their way to the hospital. They were both given
a brief examination consisting of a skull X-ray, a
peripheral-vision test, various pokings and probings and a
series of oral questions to make sure the memory and
thinking processes were not injured. There were two series
of questions. The first consisted of things like date of birth,
place of birth, parents' first names, name of grammar
school, etc. The second group contained current-events
questions like name the president, the vice-president, who
did they beat in the last election? who was the first
American in space? who held the record for most home
runs? Joe Flushing Avenue did so poorly on these that they
detained him and did some more poking and probing

before finally releasing him.

James L. Fitzsimmons, who never before had to decide whether or not to cease all relations with a client whose wake was still in progress, agreed that the wake and funeral would go on as planned, as long as Joe and Joe Flushing Avenue did *not* attend.

Changes have occurred in Joe's life before — some big ones — but they were always things he comprehended through the rearview mirror. Even getting drafted. He allowed it to happen by not accepting the fact it was happening. Uncle Sam reached out, grabbed him by the collar and dragged him to Fort Sill, Oklahoma. He wasn't the only one. It happened to everybody, didn't it? Even somewhere else he was the same kid who drank Hawaiian Punch with his macaroni. By the time he accepted the fact that his life had really changed, he was shoving a 105-millimeter shell into the open chamber of a field howitzer.

I'm gonna be someone who's not married and who does not read meters. This much he sees coming. An *un*-married *non*-meter reader. This much he is now sure of, accepts, causes. He knows, also, that his headlights do not reach beyond this.

He will struggle.

Joe leans against the fender next to Joe Flushing Avenue and asks him what he wants for lunch. He's buying.

'I ain't hungry,' Joe Flushing Avenue says.

'Ya gotta eat somethin.'

'I bet Sonny's Mass is goin on right now.'

Of all the things Joe Flushing Avenue has to be angry about, being excluded from Sonny's funeral has made him the angriest.

'It started at eleven. It could still be goin on. So whaddaya want ta eat?'

'I ain't hungry,' Joe Flushing Avenue says again. 'Why don't we go for a ride?'

'Where?' Joe asks.

'Richmond Hill.'

'Why not?' Joe says and smiles.

Right now Sonny's funeral Mass is probably just ending and the line of cars is assembling for the procession from Holy Child Jesus Church on Eighty-sixth Avenue up Lefferts Boulevard to Maple Grove Cemetery.

They get in the car and head down Myrtle Avenue toward Richmond Hill.

Joe is feeling two things which are, maybe, one thing: That the struggle he is in will take him somewhere and that this time it will not end. Maybe the place it will take him to is where he finally accepts that this is all there is.

Maybe inside the shell of your life — your heritage, living room furniture, birthmarks, bowling average, memories, fears, the nicknames your mother called you when she bounced you on her knee, your income, eating and shitting habits, what you think women see when they look at you, scars, regrets, secrets — and all the passengers: Rosie, his parents, Joe Flushing Avenue, people as seemingly unrelated as Sonny, others, pieces of others, combinations of others-all the continents on the crust of the planet you call your life...

Joe The Engineer Lazaro... This Is Your Life!

under all this shit–struggle, constant motion. If you're anything more — fuck it — you'll never know it in this life.

They stop at a red light. A young woman crossing the street looks at the white boxer shorts and smiles. Joe Flushing Avenue sticks his bandaged head out the window and sings, *'I surrender dear...'*

When they get to Lefferts Boulevard they only have a minute to wait before the procession appears.

First the hearse with Mr. Fitzsimmons in the passenger seat. Then a limousine with Mary, Sonny's mother, Sonny's two brothers and their wives. Three cars later

Johnny Lemons's '64 Buick rolls by, rocking slowly on its worn-out shocks.

Joe Flushing Avenue swings into line behind him. He taps the horn. Johnny looks through the rearview mirror, then turns around to get a better view of whoever it is behind him crazy enough to drive around with an enormous pair of undershorts flapping on the aerial. When Johnny recognizes them he smiles and waves.

An *un*-married *non*-meter reader. The farthest his headlights reach.

What else in the future?

Maple Grove Cemetery, four blocks in the future. The marquee of the Austin Theater showing *Taxi Driver* and, at midnight, *Teacher's Pet*, two blocks in the future. Sophie's Bakery, Tang's Rainwear, a laundromat with a sheet of plywood replacing a broken pane of glass in the bottom half of its front door, only one block in the future.

And the immediate future. In the immediate future is a *Visit the Grand Canyon* bumper sticker on the back of Johnny Lemons's car, probably from its last owner, with the dark silhouettes of an Indian chief on one side and a cowboy, his hat tilted forward, a cigarette drooping from his mouth, on the other.